Folktales
from
Africa

For Duncan

RETOLD BY DIANNE STEWART
ILLUSTRATED BY MARJORIE VAN HEERDEN

CONTENTS

INTRODUCTION

Before folktales were recorded in books they were *told* in order to survive in the memories of people. The storyteller, often a grandmother, chose a story from a bank of traditional tales, adjusting it according to her personality and the needs of the audience. Their participation made storytelling a communal activity. Although timeless, folktales are a product of the social, cultural and political environment in which they are told. I have shown their contemporary relevance through a Fact File that appears at the end of most folktales.

In the old Hausa folktale *Sibling Rivalry*, Hallabu goes on a journey with beautiful cloths and kola nuts as a bride price. My research showed that kola nuts are not only a favourite street food in Nigeria, but they have symbolic value when used in ritual ceremonies. The cloth referred to here was probably indigo-dyed cloth, which is still produced in Kano, northern Nigeria.

The Song of the King's Son, a Swazi folktale published in London in 1908, might seem to have limited relevance to a modern reader, but the First Fruits Festival, referred to in the tale, is still important in Swazi culture today. It is part of the Incwala or Kingship Ceremony, which takes place in December.

In *How Yams came to the Ashanti*, a tale from Ghana, you discover how this staple food of West Africa, became important in the Ashanti diet. Closer examination reveals the fact that according to Ashanti tradition, boys inherit property not from their father, but from their maternal uncle.

The Zulu folktale *The Discarded Bread* highlights the symbolic value of food, in this instance bread, in societies where people live at subsistence level. Food often represents a person's struggle for survival.

In some folktales animals show human characteristics, which allows distancing so that moral lessons about human behaviour can be taught. Because the animals in the Xhosa tale *Animals' Revenge* are old and no longer of use, they are treated poorly. This highlights the plight of the elderly who, when too old and frail to be productive, are often unwanted.

This collection of folktales drawn from the African landscape is intended for enjoyment and entertainment, but it is hoped that you will gain more insight into the countries from which the tales have been sourced.

THE ORIGIN OF STORIES

ZULU, SOUTH AFRICA

A man and his wife lived in a happy household near the sea. On a still day they could hear the roar of waves as they pounded onto the sandy beach, and on a windswept day they could see streaks of white foam riding the Indian Ocean like men on horseback.

In summer the man, his wife and children walked along the beach in the late afternoon. The mother and her children looked for shells and watched ghost crabs retreat into their holes, while the man loved to watch sea birds: the terns as they dived into the water to catch fish, the plovers as they strutted along the shore, and the migrant gulls as they scavenged for food. At home the man would carve bird and animal forms out of wood that he found, and in his home were beautiful sculptures displayed for all to see.

The family spent much time hunting, curing hides, tending the fields and weaving baskets using the materials that grew along the coast. At night, after their daily tasks, they rested around a fire under the stars.

As they watched the fire dance before them, the children begged their mother to tell them stories. 'Tell us stories!' the children nagged. *'Sifuna izinganekwane!'* (We want stories.) But the woman had no stories to tell her children. She couldn't even think of one!

Early the next morning the woman visited her neighbours to try and find stories so that she would not disappoint her children. 'We do not know any,' they said, shaking their heads. Then the woman turned her ears to the wind as it rustled the leaves of the umdoni trees and sneaked around the yard, hoping that it had stories to tell, but she heard nothing.

Every evening the children begged for stories until, in desperation, the man of the house sent his wife away in search of tales, promising to take care of the children and the household while she was away.

With the sound of the sea at her back, the woman followed the well-worn paths gouged out of the earth by people and cattle, and went in search of stories. Soon she met a hare nibbling grass at the edge of a clump of bushes. She quickly addressed the little animal, known for his trickster ways, before he disappeared into the bush.

'Do you have any stories for me, Hare? My family are desperate for tales.'

'Ooh! I have plenty of tales. So many that I have lost count,' he replied.

'Please recall some so that I can tell them to my children,' the woman said excitedly. 'They are nagging me for stories.'

'Well, I'm very busy now as you can see … and you know what happens to people who tell stories in the daytime …' Then the hare scuttled into the bushes leaving a little trail of dust.

The woman continued on her way, disappointed that the hare, who really had no stories to tell, had tricked her! As she walked along the hillside she looked out for people and animals who could tell her tales.

The summer heat was tiring and the woman decided to rest for a while in the cool forest. Before she reached the shady trees, she met Baboon and her young near an outcrop of rocks.

'I see you have children, just like me,' she said to the baboon. 'My children have sent me in search of stories for them. Do you have any to tell me, so that I can take them back to my family?'

'You want stories?' Baboon laughed. Do you think I have time for stories? I spend all my time feeding my young and keeping them safe. Your request is rather strange!'

So the woman quickly left the baboon and her family and entered the cool forest. As she looked up, she saw a wood owl perched on the branch of a

gnarled tree. She immediately tried to capture his attention by looking up at him and saying: 'Wood Owl, do you have any stories for my children?'

'Who is the noisy creature who has disturbed my sleep?' he asked angrily. 'Stories? Is that what you want? How ridiculous!' He flitted off towards a tall tree nearby, calling: 'Hoo-hu! Hoo-hu!' and the woman caught sight of his rust-red body feathers and his brown wings that were the colour of winter leaves. His cry seemed to echo his thoughts: 'Who are you? Who are you?'

The woman was disappointed by the owl's response, but she sat down in the forest to rest and she fell asleep. She dreamed of finding stories for her children and when she awoke she walked towards a clearing where she saw an elephant breaking off the leafy branch of a tree with his agile trunk.

'Elephant,' she said, 'do you have any stories for me? My people at home are desperate for stories.'

The elephant looked kindly at the woman and said: 'I don't know any stories, but you should speak to the fish eagle. He sees far and wide when he flies in the sky and I'm sure he would know where to find stories.'

Knowing that the fish eagle is found near water, the woman retraced her footsteps back towards the sea, quickening her pace. For days she scanned the skies looking for Nkwazi, the fish eagle and waited patiently to hear his distinctive cry: 'Kow, kow, kowkowkow.'

At last she saw the fish eagle circling high above the Tugela River. She ran towards him as he flew lower and when he swooped down to catch a fish from the slow-flowing water she shouted:

'Fish Eagle! Nkwazi!'

At the sound of the woman's excited cry, the fish eagle took fright and dropped the fish that he had tightly clenched in his talons. 'Plop … plop …' it sounded as it hit the brown water, which was the colour of the bulrushes that grow in the marshes near the river.

'I have lost my fish because of you!' said the fish eagle. 'What do you want?'

'I have heard that you are the great bird of the sky and that you are wise,' said the woman. 'My family need me to tell stories to them and I do not know any? Do you know where I could find some tales?'

Fish Eagle liked being referred to as wise, so he forgot about fishing and gave the woman his attention.

'I am knowledgeable about some things on earth, but not others,' he said. 'But wait! I know of someone who knows the secrets of the ocean. Wait here while I try to find him.'

Sitting on the sand at the river mouth, watching the incoming tide creep closer towards her, the woman waited for the fish eagle's return. She moved back when the high tide swept up the beach and then receded, exposing the rocks and the ghost crabs that scuttled towards the waves or disappeared down their holes

At last the fish eagle returned with news.

'There is a large sea turtle who has offered to take you to a place where you will be able to find stories,' said the fish eagle. 'Look, he is coming out of the water.'

When the woman had explained what she wanted the sea turtle said: 'Woman, climb on my back and hold my shell firmly.'

The woman was a little afraid, but she obeyed the turtle. They travelled the waves with difficulty and together they journeyed into the depths of the sea. The woman had never seen such beauty before. On and on they travelled towards the bottom of the sea, where they met the King and Queen of the Seas.

'Woman from the dry earth, what do you want from us?' they asked.

'I am looking for stories to take to my children. They are desperate for tales.'

'We have many tales, young woman, but what will you give us in return?'

'What do you desire?' the woman asked respectfully.

'We can never go to the dry earth so we would like a picture of your family, your house and your village,' said the Sea King.

'Alright,' said the woman excitedly.

Then she climbed on the turtle's back and they journeyed back through the depths of the ocean towards the land.

As she climbed off his back at the edge of the water, the woman said: 'Please come back at full moon. I will have the Sea King's gift ready by then.'

Then the young woman ran up the hill towards her home and shared her experiences with her family, telling her husband about the picture.

'I can carve a picture in exchange for stories,' he said, going out to select suitable wood for his sculpture from tree stumps and old branches that were stored nearby.

The woman was so excited that she spent many hours watching her husband sculpt, chipping away unwanted pieces until, gradually, the picture emerged. It was beautiful. When her neighbours heard about the sculpture, they all came to see the man carving and they were very excited that their village was included as well.

By the time the full moon rose in an autumn sky, the picture was complete. The man tied the picture to his wife's back as she climbed onto the back of the sea turtle.

Down, down they travelled, past seaweed and shoals of fish until they reached the King and Queen. When the young woman presented the picture to them, they were overjoyed and complimented the woman on her husband's talents.

As a token of thanks they gave the woman a shell necklace to take to her husband, and then they said to her: 'The gift of stories is given to you from us. It is for you and your people.'

Then they handed her a large shell, the most beautiful shell she had ever seen. 'When you need a story, hold this shell against your ear and you will hear a story!' they explained.

Guarding the shell protectively, the woman climbed on the turtle's back and returned to the land. Her family and people from the village lit a fire on the beach to welcome her home. The young woman had hardly put her foot on the sand when the children shouted: 'We want a story. Please tell us a tale!'

So the woman lifted the shell to her ear, holding it with both hands. She listened as the sea surged behind her. Then she began her story … *Kwasukesukela* …

THE PIG AND THE DISRESPECTFUL MAN

ZULU, SOUTH AFRICA

'*Kwasukesukela ...*' The storyteller's words took wings and excitement grew in the young audience who were seated around her.

'*Cosi, cosi*,' they replied. (Little by little.)

With the full moon behind her, the old woman began her story ...

On the north side of the Tugela River, which flows from the mighty mountains into the sea, lived a handsome young man who had a beautiful girlfriend. Both boys and girls in the area were in awe of her beauty that shone from within.

Just before dusk one day, as the setting sun cast its last light on the gently flowing landscape, the young man was walking beside the river when he saw a pig dragging itself up the river bank. It struggled to climb the slippery slope with its short legs, but when it was free, it ran towards the young man.

He was so disgusted by the sight of the pig, which dropped a smelly trail of mud behind it, that he spat on the earth in front of the pig. This offended and angered the sludge-stained pig so much that rage rose in the animal. Then it said: 'Young man, one day when a person spits at you, see how you feel!'

The handsome boy looked at the pig standing in front of him and, instead of feeling guilty about what he had done, he laughed out loud, mocking the pig.

The pig looked dejected and was saddened by the attitude of the young man who came from a respectable home.

Food was always freely available in his household and he lacked nothing. In fact, he thought so highly of himself that that he didn't believe the pig's words. He even doubted whether anyone would ever lift an eyebrow to him, let alone spit at him!

As he turned to walk away from the pig, the young man saw people walking among the shadows not far from him. They had just finished harvesting their crops in the fields and near him was a sack of corn. As he looked at it, his eyes were drawn to a brown rat, the colour of earth. He noticed its whiskers twitching as it tried to make a hole in the sack.

Impulsively the young man kicked the rat and when it landed some distance away, it was dazed.

When the poor rat came to its senses, it cried out: 'Young man, you have not lived long. One day you'll be starving like me and people will kick you away from the food you are eating, just like you did to me! You'll see what it is like!'

As the young man stared at the rat, a smile appeared on his face and he looked scornfully at the tiny animal.

'Pride comes before a fall!' said the rat as it scuttled into the long grass.

But the young man just laughed at the rat, not paying attention to its words.

When the following spring turned to summer, the young man was invited by a mediator to accompany him to his girlfriend's house. As they travelled over the hills, the mediator said to the young man: 'Listen to me, now. Do not make a pig of yourself at your future in-laws' house. You must never be greedy and overeat at their home. Do not take advantage of their hospitality.'

The young man smiled at the older man as he spoke.

'I will kick you gently when I feel that you have eaten enough. That is the signal for you to stop eating!' he said.

Soon after the two travellers' arrival at the in-laws' house, a generous meal was served and the meat and dumplings made the young man's mouth water. His long journey had made him very hungry.

While he was enjoying the meal, a dark grey cat brushed against his foot and he politely stopped eating at once, as he was instructed to do. But when he looked around, he was surprised to see that everyone else was still eating.

After eating, the visitors were told where they would spend the night and as the young man had eaten very little, he was still starving. He watched carefully to see where the pots of food were taken.

'I am so hungry,' he thought. 'I would love to eat some more of those delicious dumplings.'

As he was being led to his sleeping place, the young man thought that he would go and find the food pots when everyone was asleep. He waited impatiently until the frenetic activity of the household had died down and then, assuming that everyone was asleep, he crept quietly to the place where the pots were kept.

He looked everywhere but he couldn't find a spoon and because he was so desperately hungry, he tilted the pot directly towards his mouth, supporting it with both hands. When the hunger pangs were gone and he felt satisfied, he tried to pull his head out of the pot, but it was stuck! When he was guzzling the food, the pot's handle had slipped over his head.

The young man was frantic as he thought of ways to get himself out of his predicament, but nothing worked.

Eventually, in desperation, he decided to sit against the fence and wait until morning, bemoaning the fact that he couldn't sleep like that!

When the first barking dogs aroused the members of the household from their deep sleep, the young man felt humiliated that people would see him like that. When local people came into the yard and saw him, they sniggered and laughed out loud and invited everyone from far and wide to come and look at him. Someone spat at him and one person even tried to kick him. The handsome young man was so full of shame.

When a member of the household succeeded in pulling the pot off his head, the young man disappeared as fast as a bolt of lightning striking the earth.

This tale was told in many households and all the young people living in that region on the north bank of the Tugela River heard it. The young man's reputation was so tainted that he never found another girlfriend and he was embarrassed by the fact that the words of the pig and the rat had come true.

'*Iyaphela lapha,*' said the old woman in a hushed voice.

'*Siyabonga! Yimnandi!*' replied the children, thanking her for the story.

THE DISCARDED BREAD

ZULU, SOUTH AFRICA

It was cool at first light when the man prepared to set out on his journey on foot. Dew was still on the ground and the sun had not yet risen.

As he gazed towards the hazy hills in the distance, he heard the shrill cry of the crested barbet that sat in the flat crown tree outside his home.

'Here is bread for your journey,' said his wife. 'You have a long journey ahead of you.'

As he did not know how long he would be away, he crammed a large bag full of bread, thinking that he would need it all.

He crossed the stream and headed north in the direction of the hills that rolled towards the hazy horizon. The landscape slowly became alive with the sound of voices and the first animals woke from their sleep. It was not long before the orange sun broke through the haze and started its journey towards the west.

By mid-morning the man was hungry, so he sat down by the roadside and ate the fresh bread that his wife had given him until he felt satisfied. Then he continued along the road. But soon he grew tired of carrying the bread. The straps cut into his shoulders and the bag weighed him down.

'This heavy bag is slowing me down,' he said aloud.

As he walked he wondered what to do with it. He did not even consider the possibility that further on he might find some hungry people to give the bread to or that later he might need the bread himself. Carrying the bag was just such a burden to him as he climbed the hills and crossed the streams that all he wanted to do was get rid of it.

Then he stopped, putting the bag on the ground while he rested. Suddenly, he flung the bag of bread down the incline that fell away from the road. Down, down, down it tumbled at great speed until it finally came to rest against a rock.

Feeling lighter, the man journeyed on, noticing that the wind had sneaked up on him, whipping the grass and trees around him into uneasy motion and blowing dust into his eyes.

Meanwhile, some field mice had seen the man's bread bounce down the hill and spill out of the bag. Quickly they ran towards it and began gnawing at it in order to satisfy their hunger. They were so famished that they ate for ages and did not even leave a crumb for the ants. The countryside was dry and food had been scarce for too long.

As the man walked on, pulling his hat down over his face to shield himself from the dust, the wind played havoc with the clouds in the sky, sending them on a journey of their own. He was quite far from home when he noticed that people were digging roots to eat as their corn supplies were finished. They could not sow their seeds until the spring rains had come to saturate the iron-hard earth and soften the ground for planting.

At night the man found shelter under a tree and such was his journey that he suddenly realized that he had been travelling for many days without much food for himself. He was very hungry and his hunger had weakened him. All he could think of was food. In his mind he could picture the exact place where he had thrown away his bread. Not thinking that by then it would be stale or mouldy, the man decided to return to the place where he had discarded his bread.

Facing into the cold, biting wind, the man put one foot in front of the other as he retraced his footsteps of the past weeks. Weary and footsore, he eventually returned to the place that he recognized by the ant-heap that was there.

He immediately started looking for the bread that he had thrown away in the grass near the road, but he could not find it. 'This is the place where I threw away my bread. What could have happened to it?' he said.

As the man started walking down the hill that fell away from the road in search of his food, he became aware of loose stones in his shoes that were jabbing his feet. He sat down to remove them and as he shook his shoes he gazed around, looking for his bread. He turned rocks and stones over as he walked slowly down the hill, growing impatient when he could not find it.

Although he was weak, he was motivated by the thought that he would surely find sustenance. But when he did not find the bread he became confused. Sweat poured down his face, hunger gnawed at his stomach and he could hardly find the energy to climb back up the hill. When he reached the ant-heap he sank onto the ground and allowed his back to be supported by the mound of earth while he rested.

Then the man stood up and re-enacted the movement he had made on the day when he had thrown his bread down the hill. 'When I threw the bread away, no-one was around to see me do it,' he said. 'How could the bread have disappeared?'

A kite soared upwards in the cloudy sky above him, but he did not even notice the bird. Nothing could make his spirit soar.

Because he was feeling so famished and faint, the man decided to start the long journey home without finding his bread.

The old people say that the man is still living not far from the sea, where raffia palms flourish and the Indian Ocean sweeps up the coast towards Mozambique. They tell this story again and again, but only when there is no drought and famine, and food is plentiful. Drought and a lack of food distort a man's perception of the world. Who has ever heard of a man going back to look for bread discarded weeks earlier?

When the man came to his senses, he said: 'Difficult times do not necessarily make a man wise. I really thought that after a month I would find the bread. But I see now that difficult times distorted my view of reality. It was a foolish thing to do and I suffered a great deal as a result of my actions.'

- The Zulu nation lives mainly in KwaZulu-Natal, South Africa, and speaks isiZulu.

- The Zulu craftspeople are known for their beautiful beadwork, sculpture and basketry. The *isilulu*, a grain basket, is the largest of the Zulu baskets. Traditionally pear-shaped, it is woven from soft imbubu grass. The *isichumo*, a bottle-shaped basket used for storing liquids, has a lid that fits over the neck of the basket. It is made from the ilala palm found on the coast from the Wild Coast in the south to Maputo, Mozambique.

- Today there are modern Zulu baskets made from brightly coloured telephone wire that are used for decorative purposes.

- In Zulu folktales where humans are the main characters, they often expose the weaknesses of human nature, such as jealousy, greed or stupidity, and the folktale teaches moral lessons.

- Stories are only allowed to be told at night when the household tasks are completed. If a story is told by day, tradition dictates that the tellers may grow horns on their heads. To avoid this malady, a storyteller sometimes wears a hat with horns attached when telling a story.

- The mediator or *umkhongi* negotiates the bride price and marriage with the bride's father on behalf of the groom's father. He also ensures that the groom behaves himself.

- In a folktale where the characters are portrayed as workers in the fields, it often shows that good relationships exist. It is symbolic of a communal effort.

- Food and the lack of it have symbolic value in many African societies. Finding food on a daily basis is a problem for many people. Rather than state the problem, the situation is often portrayed by means of a narrative or story.

- The search for food is about more than survival. Symbolically it refers to the achievement of status and power. A person who has plenty of food to eat is thought of as powerful in some societies.

- People who travel are often provided with *umphako* by their family, which is food for the journey. *Padkos* (Afrikaans) would be the same thing. *Ujeqe* is traditional Zulu pot bread that is made with yeast and crushed mealies.

- The Zulu words *kwesukesukela* or *kwasuka* are similar to 'once upon a time', indicating that the folktale is about to begin. *Iyaphela lapha* (it is finished here) indicates that the story is over.

FISH BONES

XHOSA, SOUTH AFRICA

The restless sea showed its white foam teeth to the ragged rocks as it pounded onto the shore. Further inland, the wind whipped through the reeds that followed the path of the river as it snaked towards the Indian Ocean. The hills overlooking the river were home to people who complained about the cold winter.

Most days, when the weak sun was directly overhead, Nondwe walked her father's cattle to the river to quench their thirst. On one such day as she was sitting on the river bank, she began to cry when she thought of how difficult her life had become since her mother's death.

When he heard her crying, Nondwe's devoted dog came towards her wagging his tail and he licked the tears that flowed down her face. Suddenly she heard a faint voice that the wind carried towards her.

'Why are you crying?'

Startled, Nondwe looked all around, scanning the hills and river banks, but couldn't see anyone. Then she heard the words again: 'Why are you crying?'

Listening carefully, Nondwe realized that a fish was speaking the words, raising its iron-coloured head above the surface of the mud-brown river.

'I am starving,' she said in response to the fish. 'My dog and I are given very little food at home, while my father, my stepmother and her daughter Deliwe always have plenty to eat.'

'That's not right,' said the fish, thrusting his body back and forth to remain buoyant in the water. 'Wait here, child.'

Nondwe watched as the fish vanished beneath the surface of the water, leaving circular ripples in the place where it had been. Nondwe kept her eyes fixed on the water and it was not long before the fish returned with food from the depths of the river and a fish bone for her dog.

'Do not tell anyone that I have given you food,' said the fish as it disappeared from view.

Feeling satisfied by the food and stronger, Nondwe rounded up her father's cattle and headed home across the hills. She shivered as the long grass beat against her bare feet and the cold wind circled her. Tears formed in her eyes when she recalled how her unkind stepmother had given all her clothing to Deliwe, her stepsister.

She was saddened by her stepmother's unkindness to her. Her daughter, Deliwe stayed at home while Nondwe had to tend her father's cattle and goats. Because she was not fed properly, she became thinner and weaker by the day as did her dog, her only companion, as he was also not fed properly. This made her miss her own mother even more.

That night, as the cold wind rattled the windows of her house, the shivering Nondwe said: 'I'm not hungry,' when she was offered her usual supper of leftovers from Deliwe's bowl.

When the sickle-shaped moon rose in the clear, star-studded night, Nondwe and her dog could be found in the company of her father's frisky goats, which offered them warmth and comfort.

And so it was that every day when Nondwe arrived at the river with her father's fine herd of cattle, the fish brought food for her and her dog. Gradually they grew stronger and more rounded, and their ribs no longer showed through their skin.

This angered Nondwe's stepmother. When Nondwe refused to eat Deliwe's unappetising leftovers, her stepmother accused her of stealing.

'Where are you getting your food?' she asked angrily.

But Nondwe remembered the fish's request not to tell anyone that it was feeding her and she did not tell her stepmother the source of her food.

So Deliwe's mother sent her daughter to follow Nondwe and try to discover why she always refused food at home. 'What is wrong with that child?' she asked, shaking her head.

When Nondwe and the cattle trod the well-worn path to the river, Deliwe kept watch and saw the fish's head appear above the water while Nondwe was sitting on the bank above the reeds and water lilies. She marvelled at how her stepsister and her dog ate so much food and were satisfied.

When Deliwe returned home and recounted to her mother what she had seen down by the river, the unkind stepmother was very angry and devised a devious plan.

When her husband arrived home she said: 'I no longer like the food you give me. I'd love to eat some fish. Please catch me some in the morning.'

When Nondwe heard this, she was worried. At first light when the mist began to rise and dance above the surface of the water, she ran to the river and told the fish about her stepmother's plans.

'Oh!' it cried. 'That means that I will probably die.' Then the fish added, 'Child, listen carefully to my instructions.'

Nondwe drew her dog close to her and patted him. She was dismayed to think that the fish might die.

'When I have been eaten,' said the fish, 'and my bones have been thrown away, find them and keep them.'

Nondwe looked surprised. The fish continued: 'My bones will bring you both peace and contentment.'

Then the fish disappeared quickly beneath the sluggish waters of the river and Nondwe returned home.

When she returned to the river at midday to soothe the dry throats of her father's cattle with water, she noticed that he had placed his fish traps and snares at the edge of the river near the clumps of water lilies. The cold wind rustled through the reeds and chased streaks of cloud across the pale blue sky.

When she called gently to the fish, it did not come. She called again and again, but there was no response. Only the rustle of the reeds could be heard. Nondwe was so worried that something had happened to the fish.

That night, because they were very hungry, Nondwe and her dog had to accept Deliwe's leftovers. Nondwe watched uneasily as her stepmother devoured the soft flesh of the fish, taking it carefully off the bones. When she had finished eating the fish she instructed her daughter to dispose of the bones. Nondwe looked sadly at them, realizing that she had lost her friend.

Deliwe took the ivory-coloured bones and threw them onto a field not far from their house, where the Chief's son looked after his father's crops. When the young man noticed the bones lying on the soil in front of him, he tried to pick them up, but he couldn't. He bent over and tried again, but the bones slipped through his fingers.

The Chief's son then explained his predicament to his father and his councillors and they too failed to pick up the elusive fish bones.

'This is extraordinary,' said the Chief.

'Since no man is able to pick up these bones, let us see if a woman can.'

The next morning, the Chief sent a message to all the young women in the area instructing them to come and try to pick up the bones.

'Whoever succeeds will marry my son,' said the Chief, raising his arms.

Young women from far and wide travelled to the field to try and pick up the bones. The thought of becoming a royal bride greatly spurred them on. But the thin, white fish bones kept slipping out of the fingers of the maidens who tried to pick them up.

When the last young woman had failed, the Chief said: 'Has every young woman tried to solve the mystery of the bones?'

As soon as his thoughts were voiced, an old grandmother stood up and mentioned that Nondwe was not present.

'Why has she not come?' asked the Chief. 'Why was she not obedient to my request?'

'She looks after the goats and cattle of her father,' said Deliwe's mother. 'She is too shabbily dressed in rags to put in an appearance here.'

'I will not give up,' said the Chief, 'until every young woman has tried to lift the bones.'

When summoned, Nondwe came before the Chief, dressed in rags.

'It's your turn to try,' said one of the Chief's councillors.

As she bent over to pick up the slippery white fish bones, they jumped into her hands and stayed there. Amazed, she looked down at the fine bones that criss-crossed her palms. Then she offered them to the Chief.

For the first time in many years joy rose in Nondwe and she looked forward to a hopeful future.

ANIMALS' REVENGE

XHOSA, SOUTH AFRICA

The ash-coloured donkey tugged at a clump of tough grass that refused to give way. As he persevered, he could hear the distant waves crashing onto the rocky shores of the Wild Coast, sounding like thunder.

Ndlebende thought of happier times when food was plentiful and he was well cared for. For many years he had carried the ever-increasing weight of his owner and he had borne heavy loads on his back, especially at harvest time. But his legs were no longer strong enough for work so he was given poor grazing, unlike the other productive animals. His pride was hurt when he overheard his owner say: 'That donkey is so lazy. All he does is eat the grazing that should be for the cows. I will have to put him down tomorrow.'

The donkey was filled with sadness and fear, and when night threw its black blanket over the earth, the donkey set off in search of a better life. 'I am safer away from here,' he said aloud.

Ndlebende walked a long way across the grassy plains taking him away from the cliffs and Indian Ocean that swirled at their feet, until he was so tired that he lay down to rest. When light brought the countryside to life, the donkey rose and continued on his way, not quite sure where he was going. As he climbed a hill, he met a dog.

'It is such a warm, sunny day,' the donkey said to the dog. 'Why do you look so sad?'

'Today I heard my owner say that because of my age and poor hearing, he no longer wants me,' said the dog. 'He says that I cannot go hunting anymore or scare thieves.'

'I have the same problem,' said the donkey, showing his teeth. 'Come with me. We will try and start a new life.'

As the donkey and the dog walked through the forest, their feet crunched the dry leaves on the ground. Suddenly they heard a pitiful cry and when they searched the undergrowth they found a thin, scrawny cat hiding in the bushes. Nervously, it retreated when it saw them.

'What are you doing here?' asked Ndlebende.

'Sh!' whispered the cat. 'I'm hiding. When I was sleeping next to the warm fire last night I heard my owner say that because I can no longer earn my keep by catching rats, they were going to get rid of me.'

'That's sad,' said the donkey.

'I only just escaped,' said the black cat, arching its back as it stretched.

'Why don't you join us?' said the dog. 'We are all in the same position and we are looking for greener pastures.'

The three journeyed through the dappled shade of the forest, resting in the shade of a large tree with spreading branches when the sun was at its fiercest. Suddenly the throaty crowing of a rooster who had perched on a branch overhead startled them.

'Why are you living so far away from man?' asked the donkey.

'Did you not see someone chasing me while you were journeying here?' asked the rooster anxiously. 'I heard my owner say that I was about to be put in the pot!'

'No,' said the cat, looking around.

'Yes … the pot of water on the fire was already boiling!'

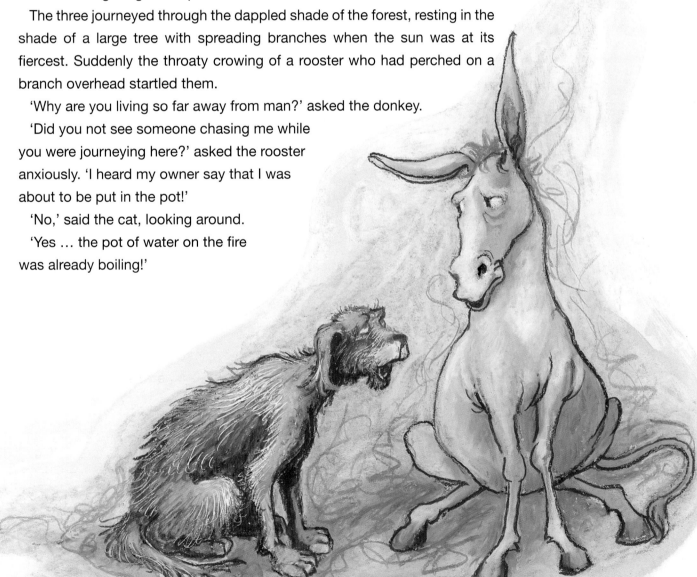

'That's terrible,' said the dog.

'But we have also fled from our homes because of our age. Journey with us, Rooster, and we will all enjoy our old age together in a place where our owners will not find us,' suggested Ndlebende.

The donkey, the dog, the cat and the rooster walked slowly on in search of a new home. When night replaced day, they rested under a tree. Owls hooted above them, but neither the weary dog and the donkey that lay on the hard earth under the gnarled tree nor the cat and rooster that slept soundly in the tree heard them.

Sometime during the night the rooster woke and saw a light in the distance. 'Wake up,' he said, but the animals slept soundly.

When he told the animals about it, they asked the cat to go and investigate, as the animals were cold and hungry. So the cat crept towards the gentle light that lit the path toward the house. On his return the cat said: 'That was a wicked place. There were bones on the floor.'

'We could always drive the humans out of their house so that we could live there!' suggested the donkey.

So the shivering animals devised a plan. Ndlebende would put his front legs up on the wall near the door, the dog would sit on the donkey's back and the cat would sit on top of the dog. Then the rooster would sit on top of the cat's head.

'Then we will scream as loudly as we can and the owners will be so frightened that they will run away immediately!'

The plan was successful. The owners of the house were so frightened by the thunderous roar that they ran back into the darkness of the night without even entering the house.

'Now, when they come back into their house, we'll all be hiding there and attack them from inside,' said the rooster.

The animals sniffed around looking for food and, after satisfying their hunger, they found their hiding places. The cat curled up next to the dying fire, the rooster balanced on top of the door that was half open, and the dog and donkey stood behind the door.

Sometime later there was a rumble of footsteps as the dangerous men returned to their house. When the first man entered, he saw the cat's sparkling eyes and mistook them for a glowing ember of the fire. When he bent over to blow the fire back into life, the cat sprang at him. Then the dog gripped his legs with his teeth and when he turned around he felt the donkey's

stone-hard hooves. As he ran out of the door, the rooster perched on his head, digging his claws into his head.

Crying and wailing, the man ran from his house, never to return to the danger that lurked there and the other men followed him as they fled from that place.

So it was that Ndlebende, the dog, the cat and the rooster lived in peace in their own little house until the end of their days.

- Former President of South Africa and Nobel Peace Prize recipient, Nelson Rolihlala Mandela, is Xhosa. He was born in Transkei on 18 July 1918 in a village near Umtata.

- Prominent Xhosa African National Congress politicians include President Thabo Mbeki and the late Steve Biko, a political activist during the apartheid era.

- The AmaXhosa speak isiXhosa and although they live throughout South Africa, they are mostly found in the Eastern Cape Province.

- The AmaXhosa are well known for their beadwork. From as early as 1820 they used glass beads imported from Europe by merchants, although in modern times plastic beads are often used. Both females and males adorned themselves with beadwork.

- White beads dominate Xhosa beadwork and are associated with purity and mediation. The colour white has ritual importance amongst the AmaXhosa. The young men undergoing initiation rituals (male circumcision) and women breastfeeding their babies put white clay on their bodies to indicate that they are undergoing these rituals.

- Traditionally, AmaXhosa men and women smoked tobacco in beautifully beaded long-stemmed pipes.

- Cattle are symbolic in Xhosa society. Traditionally the cattle were the responsibility of the father of a family. His sons helped him and women were not involved with the cattle. Cattle were a means of economic exchange and for measuring wealth. Cattle were and still are used as a bride price or lobola, paid by the groom to the parents of the girl he wishes to marry.

- In his book *The Ama-Xhosa: Life and Customs*, J.H. Soga uses special Xhosa terms to describe the shape of cattle horns and colours. *Emanqindi* (fists) describes horns that have been made blunt to avoid damage. *Epemvu* is the name given to white-faced cattle that are black or red, while *elubelu* refers to cream-coloured cattle.

- *Animals' Revenge* might have been inherited and adapted from a story told by a European missionary, but the people consider this story their own as it has been passed from generation to generation. The dangerous men referred to in *Animals' Revenge* are probably ogres who feature predominantly in African folktales. Their behaviour creates suspense. Here, the animals play the role of the trickster, performing a trick on a naïve, unsuspecting victim.

MANTIS AND THE SPRINGBOK

BUSHMAN/SAN

Mantis was used to digging holes in the hot desert sand in order to find precious water to satisfy his thirst. But this time the small San man was diligently digging to find the honey of wild bees.

The soft, warm honey trickled down his fingers as he broke pieces off the honeycomb to taste. Then he gave some to the little springbok who was resting on the mound of earth that had come from the hole.

After a while some elephants sauntered towards Mantis and when they reached the hole, one of the female elephants picked up the little springbok with her trunk and placed the African antelope on her back. Then she joined the herd that had wandered off, leaving her little elephant calf standing near the pile of sand.

'This honey is so good,' said Mantis. 'Are you eating it as well?'

But there was no reply.

Mantis repeated his question from deep down in the hole. He wondered why the little springbok was not answering.

'Kurru!' said the elephant calf.

'I cannot understand the sounds you are making,' said Mantis, breaking off some more waxy honeycomb that dripped honey.

He threw it out of the hole and said: 'Are you eating the flavourful honey?'

'Kurru!' replied the elephant calf.

Surprised by the sound, Mantis climbed out of the hole and saw the calf, and he noticed that the sand he had dug out of the hole had covered the young elephant. He dusted the elephant calf off and sent it away.

Then, looking closely at the ground, Mantis noticed the elephant tracks that circled the hole and then went away from it. He realized they must have taken the little springbok with them and left the elephant calf in his place.

He took his bone-tipped poison arrows and decided to go in search of the antelope. Then he realized that he needed to tell his sister, the little springbok's mother, that he was going to try and find her child.

'While I was digging for honey the elephants passed by and they have taken the little springbok,' said Mantis apologetically.

'Surely you would have heard them, Mantis?' said his sister.

'I was digging deep down in the hole,' he replied.

'You didn't hear the elephants because you were probably asleep down the hole,' she said angrily. 'Go at once to find my child.'

She then packed some meat for Mantis to eat on his journey and as he left her house he said: 'Watch the grass when I am away. The wind will blow the grass away from the house when I am travelling in that direction, but when I am on my way home, the wind will blow the grass towards you.'

Mantis' sister listened attentively as he spoke.

'The wind that blows from the east will blow the grass towards you and you will know that I am returning with your child.'

With the scorching sun beating down on his back, Mantis tracked the elephants, following their trail along the desert sand that burned his feet. At the crest of a hill he saw the elephants and little Springbok playing with their young. He was so delighted to see little Springbok that he ran towards him.

'My little Springbok, my pet,' said Mantis excitedly.

But when the female elephant saw Mantis she was afraid and she picked up little Springbok with her trunk and swallowed him.

'Where is little Springbok now?' said Mantis approaching the herd.

'I do not know,' said the female elephant.

'But I saw him here playing with the calves and then I saw you put him into your mouth. Springbok's mother wants him back,' said Mantis.

'What are you going to do about it?' said the female elephant.

'I will climb into your mouth and get him!' suggested Mantis.

'I'll spit you out of my mouth,' she said.

The other elephants ambled over to hear the discussion that took place between the female elephant and Mantis.

Mantis was quiet as he thought of a plan to get the little springbok back. He decided that he would get inside the female elephant through her navel. As he moved towards her, the other elephants became agitated and jabbed him with their spears, but he still managed to get into the female elephant.

Inside the elephant, Mantis retrieved the little antelope and tied him to his back with a skin. But as he came out of the elephant, the rest of the herd were waiting to attack him. Just then, the female elephant fell over and died.

Mantis feared for his life and so he grew feathers so that he could fly away with the little springbok.

Meanwhile Mantis' sister kept looking at the movement of the grass near her home. An east wind scattered the desert sand and blew the grass in the direction of her house.

'The wind is blowing towards me,' she said excitedly. 'Mantis is coming home! I hope he has found little Springbok.'

In the distance, she saw Mantis carrying the little springbok on his back and she rushed out to meet them. She was delighted to see her child and made sure that he never strayed from her sight again.

- Dr Wilhelm Bleek and his sister-in-law, Dr Lucy Lloyd, originally recorded this folktale in 1910. Their research was aided by a Cape San man named //Kabbo, who lived with them in Cape Town.

- The Bushmen or San people, one of the earliest inhabitants of southern Africa, were traditionally hunters and gatherers. The women gathered plants for food and the men hunted. Bushmen were always on the move, dependent on game, plant material and water for survival. Bushmen can run for hours at a time while tracking antelope.

- 'Mantis' (which is sometimes referred to by the Bushman name Kaggen) is a creature in Bushman folklore that has supernatural powers, yet sometimes does stupid things, showing human qualities.

- The rock art of the San or Bushmen is highly symbolic. Some of it represents the visions of the shaman-artist when in a trance. The eland, one of the largest antelope in southern Africa, was regarded as a symbol of supernatural potency or power and is often featured on rock sites in the Drakensberg in KwaZulu-Natal.

- Some of the earliest rock paintings in southern Africa are thought to be about 27 000 years old.

- The Kamberg Rock Art Centre in KwaZulu-Natal, which is open to the public, enables guests to learn more about the numerous San/Bushmen paintings found in the Ukhahlamba-Drakensberg Park, which has been declared a World Heritage Site.

- The San languages belong to the Khoisan language family. The Khoisan languages use an alphabet based on Latin characters, and the click sounds are represented by symbols such as //, ! and /.

- Today, some Bushmen or San live in the Kalahari Desert in Botswana and Namibia, and nearby Angola.

THE SONG OF THE KING'S SON

SWAZI, SWAZILAND

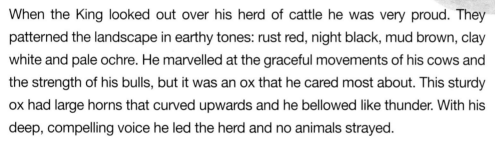

When the King looked out over his herd of cattle he was very proud. They patterned the landscape in earthy tones: rust red, night black, mud brown, clay white and pale ochre. He marvelled at the graceful movements of his cows and the strength of his bulls, but it was an ox that he cared most about. This sturdy ox had large horns that curved upwards and he bellowed like thunder. With his deep, compelling voice he led the herd and no animals strayed.

The King entrusted the care of his cattle to his son, who looked after them as if they were his own. By day the King's son took the cattle to graze in the valley near the slow-flowing river and by night they returned to their enclosure, which was surrounded by a very strong branch fence so that no-one could steal them.

During the summer, when the tall grass swayed in the breeze and almost hid the cattle from view, the herdsman had to climb on a tall rock in order to keep watch over his animals. Large rocks and boulders littered the valley and the shade they provided was cool enough for the growth of delicate ferns, while lizards basked on the hot surfaces of the rocks, catching flies.

The hot sun tired the herdsman and drained him of his strength. He longed to sleep, but he knew that he would be in trouble if his father's cattle were lost. One such day as he was watching the animals graze languidly in the valley, an old woman stopped to talk to him.

'I am so afraid that someone might steal these cattle,' he said, 'so I watch over them very carefully.'

Then the old woman pointed to a large round boulder nearby that was as smooth as the head of a bald man.

'That rock is yours,' she smiled as she spoke to the King's son.

'Because it is so smooth, no-one can climb on it without slipping off.'

'Well, how am I going to climb it then?' asked the boy.

'You will be able to and you will be safe there. But be careful not to fall asleep on the rock or your cattle will go missing.'

Then she took a breath and said: 'Listen to this song: "Cattle, cattle, come to me …"'

The King's son caught the melody and then repeated it twice to himself.

After that, whenever he wanted to round up his animals he sang this song and the cattle came to him and obediently followed him home.

One midsummer's day when the heat was so intense that the horizon seemed to quiver and the King's son was overcome by lethargy, he fell asleep on the warm round rock. His ever-watchful enemies crept over the mountain when they noticed that he was asleep. Quickly they drove the cattle away.

When the King's son awoke, he noticed that the grassy plains were bare and although he sang the cattle song, no cattle appeared. For the rest of the day he walked all through the valley searching for his father's animals until the sun slid behind the mountain and dusk fell on the land, prompting him to return home.

'Don't come back home unless you return with my cattle,' said the King angrily. 'How could you have been so careless with them?'

The King's son was so distraught that he went out into the half-moon lit night and sought refuge on his rock. He cried when he realized what he had done. 'How could I have fallen asleep?'

Suddenly he heard a scuffle and when he looked around he saw the old woman. It was dark and he did not recognize her until she spoke.

'Do you remember I told you not to sleep on the rock?'

'Yes,' replied the King's son.

'Well, what I predicted has come true. Because you fell asleep your cattle are gone.'

'I know,' said the boy. 'I cannot find them.'

'Don't worry,' said the old woman. 'Go and ask the Chief who has taken your cattle if you can work for him.'

The King's son left immediately and by moonlight he followed the narrow, steep contour paths over the mountains and across streams, guided by the moon and stars above him.

When the sun sent out its first rays, he arrived at the house of his father's enemy and heard the lowing of his father's cattle.

He approached the Chief who made him herdsman of his cows, bulls and oxen and when he took them out to pasture each day he sang the song: 'Cattle, cattle, come to me!' No animals ever strayed and when they heard the song, they came back to him. The boy worked for the Chief for many years until he was a man. All the time he devised plans for returning home with his father's cattle.

At the time of the First Fruits Festival, men and women harvested their first ripe maize and sorghum, and the children went out gathering firewood. There was no-one at home except for an old woman and the King's son. The women had made beer in calabashes that were placed in a row and, creeping quietly up to the containers, the King's son took a herb that induces sleep and ground it into a fine powder. Then he sprinkled some in each calabash.

'This will put them to sleep,' he said aloud.

Later, the celebrations began. The Chief sat under a canopy of green branches and the first fruits were brought to him. A small branch from each gift was placed around his neck or arms. Then the Chief slowly drank a mixture of seawater and herbs, which he gave to all, signalling the start of the feast.

Those gathered there ate the freshly harvested corn and nuts, and drank the beer, except for the King's son. Then all present sunk into a deep sleep and no-one saw the rising of the full moon in a cloudless sky.

The King's son crept away and quickly opened the gate of the cattle enclosure, being careful that his movements were not heard. He sang: 'Cattle, cattle, come to me!' and the animals rose to their feet and followed their herdsman, straight past the sleeping men. When they had gone some distance, the ox with the horns turned inwards bellowed loudly and all the cattle in the neighbouring areas followed him as well.

At dawn when the men forced their eyes open and found that not only their cattle but all the cattle in the surrounding areas had gone, the Chief immediately suspected his herdsman and sent his men after him. Because cattle walk slowly, especially over rugged, rocky terrain, the Chief's men had caught up with the King's son by dusk of the second day.

He was so afraid when he saw his father's enemy approaching that he guided his animals down the slopes of the mountain to the banks of a stream where thorn trees were silhouetted in the fading light.

Strong wild figs with monkey ropes hanging down and thick bushes offered some protection from the night, but the herdsman did not know how he was going to save the cattle.

As he hid under the wild fig tree, crouched against its trunk, loud croaking frogs, murmuring crickets and buzzing gnats drowned his thoughts. He feared that at dawn the enemy would close in on him and he would lose the cattle. Then a bat swooped low, brushing against his head and as he raised his hand to protect himself, he caught sight of the old woman.

'Do not be afraid,' she whispered. 'Obey me and you will come to no harm. Kill a white ox, skin it and make 10 000 little white shields out of the hide.'

The King's son was startled by her suggestion.

'Then I will find you soldiers.'

He did what he was told and then he heard the woman say: 'Frogs! You that hide underneath the stones! Take these shields and do what the King's son commands!'

The young man gave the shields to the frogs and instructed them by the light of the moon. When he cried: 'Woo-ooh!' they were to rise up and shout with their shields in front of them and when he said: 'Boo-ooh!' they were to retreat and hide.

Before night changed to day, the King's son lined up the frogs in a long row with their shields in front of them at a place where they would be visible to the enemy. When the enemy first appeared, the frogs rose, held up their shields and shouted: 'Woo-ooh!' It seemed as though thunder had broken the silence of the morning.

The enemy were so afraid that they retreated, telling their Chief that there was an army of several thousand across the stream. The Chief sent more men who returned with the same story and when he sent his army they said: 'Rather let us lose our cattle than our lives.' The dejected Chief then ordered everyone to return home.

The King's son was so relieved. He thanked the frogs, herded his cattle together and journeyed home. The King was so pleased to see him and his cattle that he gave his son a wife and made him chief of all his sons.

Every night as darkness covered the land the King's son sang his song to the cattle: 'Cattle, cattle come to me!', which kept them safe.

- The government of Swaziland is a monarchy. In a monarchy, one person, usually a king or queen rules and is often the head of the state, not the government, and the ruler's right to reign is usually hereditary.

- The main industries are sugar and wood pulp, and the mining of coal and asbestos. Maize is the most cultivated grain.

- In folktales where humans and animals appear in the same tale, there is often an element of fantasy where the animal is unusually powerful.

- The Malolotja Nature Reserve in Swaziland is an important breeding ground for the blue swallow, bald ibis and blue crane, which are endangered species.

- This folktale, originally recorded in 1908, refers to the First Fruits Festival.

- The Incwala or Kingship Ceremony, of which the First Fruits Festival is a part, is still celebrated in Swaziland today in December and is a time when the King is revered. The first part involves the Bemanti or 'water people' going to Mozambique to collect foam from the waves of the Indian Ocean, which is believed to have healing powers. Their return is marked by the Little Incwala, which consists of dancing, ritual and singing. As part of the main Incwala, youth from all over Swaziland meet at a venue with branches from the precious Lusekwane bush, which are made into a structure that forms the King's special enclosure. On the third day a bull is traditionally slaughtered and on the fourth day the King and warriors dress in full ceremonial attire. On this day the King tastes produce from the first harvest. These symbolic rituals end with a fire a few days later, marking the end of the old year.

- The Umhlanga Reed Dance is an important ceremony held every year. This ceremony symbolizes the young unmarried maidens' loyalty to the kingdom of Swaziland.

- The smooth rock referred to in this story may have been a granite rock. The world's largest granite rock is found near Mbabane, Swaziland's capital, and is called Sibebe Rock.

THE LONELY GOAT-HERDER

SOTHO, LESOTHO

The first light of morning highlighted the crags and crevasses of the rocky mountains of Lesotho that rose in jagged ridges to reach the sky that arched above them. It was a calm, still day.

A lammergeyer glided through the air, alert to the possibility of food and its whistling cry was heard by Molisa-oa-Lipoli as she opened the enclosure to let out the goats for grazing. As she followed them through the grass that was still wet with dew, she thought of all the tasks that she had to do at home. Grinding the corn was a daily activity and she had to cook porridge for everyone in the household. She was seldom given much herself and had to feed herself by licking the porridge spoon. She often felt pangs of hunger when she was out on the windy hillside with the goats.

The people with whom she lived were unkind to her. They often chased her away and some boys threw stones at her. But there was one kind person who cared deeply for Molisa and that was her old grandmother, who was bent over with age. When she was out on the hills, Molisa's grandmother walked far distances to bring her food.

One autumn day, when the people chased Molisa away, she decided to go and hide where no-one would find her. She ran as fast as a hare, ignoring the stitch in her side until she was so exhausted that she decided to sit down

and rest. A brisk wind arose, which swirled around the mountains and unsettled the dust, making Molisa's eyes sting.

She had just finished rubbing her eyes when she noticed that a bowl of food had been placed beside her. Although she was famished, she was very suspicious as she thought that she might be poisoned if she ate the food so she decided to continue on her journey, leaving the food behind. As she walked along the stony mountain paths she thought longingly of all the times that she was out with her frisky goats, which were wonderful companions to her. She saw few animals or people along the way and that evening she was so hungry and exhausted from the journey that she sat down and cried. When she stopped crying she saw a bowl of food at her side and she decided to try a little of it. When nothing happened to her, she ate more until she had satisfied her hunger.

Molisa slept soundly that night beneath the stars and when the sun woke her the next morning she was relieved to discover that she was still alive.

To her surprise she found another bowl of food at her side, which she ate hungrily before she continued on her journey. All day she travelled until she came to a steep mountain where she saw a small house that was partially hidden by a screen of reeds placed in front of it.

Cautiously she crept towards the house and nervously looked behind the screen. When she peered into the house she noticed that no-one was there. Then she sat against the wall of the house, basking in the sun like a lizard. Molisa wondered where the owners were. Were they working in their fields? Suddenly she noticed a bowl of food at her side and a clay pot full of water, probably from the stream nearby. Molisa jumped up, poured the cool water over her grimy hands and then devoured the food.

That evening, when cold seeped into the land between the mountains, Molisa noticed that a fire had been kindled nearby. Embraced by the warmth of the glowing embers, she fell asleep next to the fire. When the first bird calls woke her the next day she found that she was lying on a sleeping mat on the floor of the house and skin blankets had been placed over her.

When Molisa stood up and stretched, she noticed a pile of clothes on the floor. Quickly she tried them on and to her delight she discovered that they fitted her perfectly. Then she put beads around her neck and bands that glistened in the bright sunlight on her arms and legs. When she looked for her old, ragged clothes, she saw the remnants of them in the fire and, as she danced in her new clothes, she felt like the wife of a *morena* (chief).

From that time, the goat-herder lived the live of a *morena's* wife. She did not have to work as her tasks were done for her, even the sweeping. But Molisa was so desperately lonely that her heart ached. Not even the beauty of the mountains that protected her could uplift her. She longed for human company. She missed her grandmother and her goats.

In time, the hands that cared for her gave her a son. She was overjoyed, but she longed to show her son to someone. Then she remembered her old grandmother who lived over the mountains, the one with kind, smiling eyes and wrinkles on her face like furrows, and she decided to visit her.

It was a long journey and when she arrived at her old home with her son in the *thari* (sling) on her back, the villagers couldn't believe what they saw.

'Such beautiful clothes,' they smirked. 'Where did she get them?'

'She even walks like a *morena's* wife!' they commented.

Molisa walked confidently past the villagers and members of her household until she saw her grandmother who came out to greet her.

'I need someone to help me care for my son,' she said to her grandmother.

'I will find someone for you,' she replied and offered Molisa a place to stay.

A few days later Molisa and her helper climbed the hills and crossed the streams, encouraging each other as they walked the long distance back to Molisa's house. With someone to care for her child, Molisa dreamed of cultivating a field for herself against the mountain where she could grow pumpkins, corn, sweet reeds and watermelons.

'I need a hoe to break the iron-hard earth,' she said to her helper.

The following morning Molisa thought she was dreaming when the first light revealed a hoe resting against the wall of her house and seeds for her to use.

Molisa was so excited as she began to prepare her field for planting and when she had used all her seeds, she sent her helper back to her old home to ask for more seeds to plant. When her helper was away, Molisa spent time weeding the fields and fetching water from the stream to water the plants that had just appeared above the ground.

On her return, the young girl was surprised to see that there were other houses near her own with men, women and children living in them. Hens strutted through the yards and there were enclosures for the cattle.

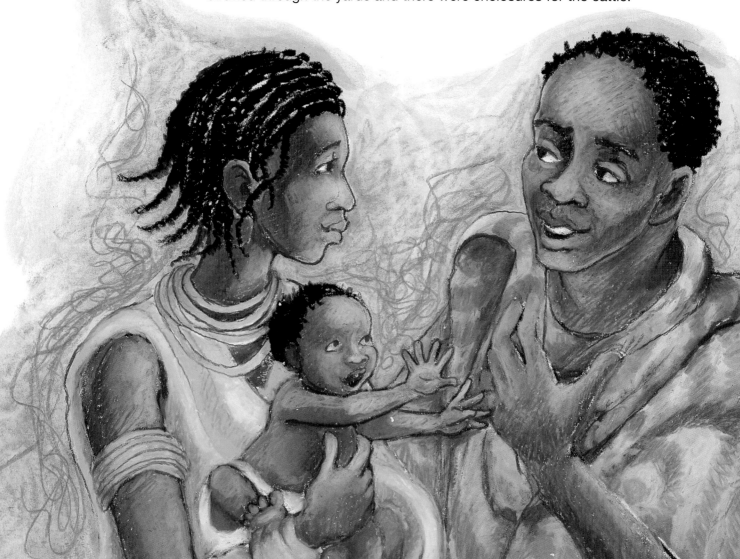

When Molisa returned from her field that evening, she, too, was surprised to see that the mountain slope had so many houses on it and when she approached her house she saw a handsome young man sitting inside the reed screen.

'Where is your husband?' he asked.

'I do not have one. I only have a child,' Molisa replied.

'I am your husband,' said the man. 'And this is my child.'

Molisa was startled, but when she looked at her child she noticed that he resembled the good-looking young man and she was pleased to see that there was an affinity between the young man and her son.

Molisa and her husband, the Chief, were very contented, but they were sad that Molisa's own family had been unkind to her and that they had been allowed to get away with their bad behaviour.

The seasons changed and, at the time of the harvest, the Chief collected corn, plenty of wheat and sorghum and he stored it underground. But then a drought crept into the mountain kingdom and news reached Molisa that her family had been badly affected and were without food.

So the Chief sent a message back to them offering them food in exchange for cattle.

When the people arrived with their grass baskets and leather bags, the Chief noticed how thin they were and he gave them enough food to satisfy their hunger. Then he ordered his men to fill their bags. But their bags were stuffed full of dung, except for Molisa's grandmother's bag, which was filled with grain.

It was only when the people returned home with their heavy loads that they realized that there was no food in their bags and they were very angry as they had carried them over the rocky terrain with great difficulty.

'This is terrible,' the people cried. 'We have been tricked. We cannot continue to live in a place where there is no food. We will have to go to a place over the mountains where there is a good supply of food for our needs.'

So the members of Molisa's household left that place on a night when the thin crescent moon that resembled the horns of a cow hung suspended in the sky. Only Molisa's grandmother remained behind. After a few days had passed, Molisa sent a messenger to fetch her grandmother, who lived in a new house built for her and Molisa cared for her until she died.

- The kingdom of Lesotho gained its independence in 1966 and is a landlocked country surrounded by South Africa.
- Maseru is the capital city.
- The Maluti Mountains, an extension of the Drakensberg Mountains reach a height of just under 3 000 metres.
- Lesotho is populated by the Basotho, who speak Sesotho.
- Industries include tourism (pony-trekking through the mountains is popular), textiles, construction and crafts.
- *Motoho* is the traditional porridge.
- The Basotho hat is a national emblem of the country.
- Traditionally, the Basotho have always worn blankets, both in everyday life and on ceremonial occasions and have a variety to suit different occasions. Men fasten their blankets at the right shoulder, allowing them to use their right arm, while women tend to fasten their blankets midway across the chest.
- There is a high wool content in the blankets, which is beneficial in wet weather, as wool does not absorb too much water.
- The use of the blanket is symbolic. A newly married woman wears a shawl around her hips until she falls pregnant with her first child. When born, the baby is ritually wrapped in a chosen blanket, which is then used to tie the baby to the mother's back.
- Often a husband gives a wife a wedding blanket and it may also be part of *bohali*, the bride price.
- When a boy undergoes initiation, he acquires a new blanket, indicating his rite of passage from boyhood to manhood.
- A blanket is often given as a gift when a person goes on a journey.

THE CLEVER MAN AND THE FOOLISH MAN

BAKONGO, ANGOLA

All eyes were focused on the storyteller as he began to tell his tale.

One spring morning, two brothers went to the mangrove swamp just as the tide was receding in order to catch fish. It was their duty to find food for their parents.

As the water level dropped and the roots of the trees were reflected in the still, calm surface of the water, the boys took up their position at the edge of the water and started looking for fish.

Suddenly the one brother, who was known as Foolish Man, noticed a circle of ripples disturb the water and he saw a fish swimming just beneath the surface. He immediately fired at it, killing the fish. Clever Man, the other brother, also fired soon afterwards, but his shot was not aimed at anything and it did not hit anything either.

'Foolish Man,' said his brother, running towards him, 'have you caught any fish yet?'

'I may be a fool,' he replied, 'but yes, Clever Man, I did get a fish.'

Then Clever Man said: 'But you are so foolish, Foolish Man, you don't understand.'

Clever Man continued his explanation. 'When I fired, I hit the fish and it swam towards you. So actually, the fish you have is mine.'

Foolish Man looked at him, shaking his head in disbelief.

'Please give it back to me,' said Clever Man.

Foolish Man could not understand why it was his brother's, but he gave the fish to his brother anyway.

The two brothers then walked home and Clever Man gave the fish to his father saying: 'This is what I shot. Your foolish son came home with nothing.'

The father smiled approvingly at Clever Man and the boys' mother cooked the fish for supper. The father and Clever Man ate heartily, commenting on the fine taste of the fish. But they offered none to Foolish Man.

The next day when the tide was right and the waters had gone down enough, the two brothers went to fish again at the mangrove swamp. It was not long before Foolish Man (who had a good eye) fired and killed a huge fish with the first pull of the trigger.

'Didn't you hear the shot?' Clever Man asked his brother.

'Yes, that was my shot,' said Foolish Man.

'Look, there is the fish that I shot,' said Clever Man, pointing to it.

Although baffled, Foolish Man said: 'You may have the fish then'

When they arrived home at the close of the day, the boys' mother was so excited to see the fish that they had brought home with them.

'It is large,' she said. 'It will make a good meal.'

She then prepared and cooked the fish with seasonings and gave the flavourful meal to Clever Man and his father, but none was given to Foolish Man, who sat silently watching his family eat.

As they were eating and commenting on the fine flesh of the fresh fish, a fish bone got stuck in the father's throat. He was choking and everyone ran around him, looking very worried.

'Quick, Foolish Man. Go and get a doctor,' said Clever Man.

'No, I cannot,' said Foolish Man. 'Something might happen when I'm gone.'

'Your father's health is in danger, Foolish Man. Do as I say.'

But Foolish Man sang a song:

'It is my fish you eat every day,
I shot the fish that came my way;
You call me foolish
And you give me no fish.'

Clever Man was angry. 'How can you waste time singing when your father needs help? Aren't you concerned about his suffering? He might die. Hurry, go and get the doctor. Father needs your help, Foolish Man.'

But Foolish Man took no notice of his brother's words and continued to sing quietly:

'You eat and eat until you are satisfied,
A fish bone gets caught in your throat.
And now your life is nearing its end
With the bone still in your throat.'

Clever Man was clearly irritated. 'Can't you see that father needs help? Go and fetch the doctor!' But Foolish Man continued singing:

'Clever Man, did you who killed the fish,
Give your brother anything to eat in a dish?
No! Look what has happened.
Perhaps, you wish that you had given
Foolish Man something to eat.'

The boys' mother stood by helpless and as Foolish Man finished singing his song, his father died. The neighbours and members of the community came to the house when they heard the sad news about the boys' father and they asked how Foolish Man could possibly continue with his singing when his father had just died.

But Foolish Man replied: 'Our father created both of us brothers. One is a clever man and the other is a fool. I, the fool, killed the food and they ate it, giving none to me. They took advantage of me.'

The villagers shook their heads in disbelief.

'People must not blame me if I continue to sing while they are mourning. I starved while they had more than enough to eat,' said Foolish Man.

The people discussed the matter amongst themselves and decided that Foolish Man was in the right and they went away shaking their heads. They believed that the father received his just reward for not feeding Foolish Man.

'The one who eats oily fish will suffer indigestion,' said the storyteller.

'And that ends my story … Oh! Perhaps tomorrow you should go and chop palm kernels rather than fish!' he said smiling.

- Angola is situated on the west coast of Africa, between the Democratic Republic of the Congo in the north and Namibia in the south.
- Angola is struggling to recover from the 27-year civil war that raged in the country after it gained its independence from Portugal in 1975. The MPLA (Popular Movement for the Liberation of Angola) and the rebel group, Unita, were enemies before Angola gained independence.
- Angola is one of the major oil producers in Africa.
- Luanda is the capital.
- Portuguese is the official language. Other languages spoken include Umbundu, Kimbundu and Kikongo, spoken by the Bakongo.
- The Bakongo people (also know as the Kongo) live along the west (Atlantic) coast of Africa between Pointe-Noire, Congo (Brazzaville) and Luanda, Angola. They are also found in Congo (Kinshasa).
- The Bakongo comprise about 15 per cent of the population in Angola.
- The Bakongo grow maize, sweet potatoes, cassava, bananas, peanuts and beans. Their cash crops include coffee, cacao, palm oil and bananas.
- Fishing and hunting is still practised by the Bakongo, but many live and work in towns.
- Extensive areas of mangrove forests occur around Luanda.

FACT FILE

SIBLING RIVALRY

HAUSA, NIGERIA

There was once a man living in northern Nigeria who longed for a daughter. Although he was very proud of his two sons, Hallabu and Shadusa, he was delighted when his wife gave birth to a girl.

When he went to the market he bought her fine hand-woven cloth and beautiful beads to wear around her neck, but he gave little to his sons, even on feast days. This young girl did not even have to work like the other girls in the village. Her father ordered her brothers to collect firewood and water for their home.

As she grew into a beautiful young girl, her two brothers grew jealous of her and all the attention she received from their father.

One spring morning, when she was about ten years old, her eldest brother Hallabu said: 'Please help us to gather firewood in the forest today. We'll climb the trees and break off the branches. All you have to do is tie the wood into bundles. You'll really help us if you do.'

The young girl agreed and eagerly set off for the forest with her brothers, passing her father's fields of cassava, millet and sorghum that had recently been planted. It was cool and shady in the forest and the young girl willingly helped her brothers with their tasks. When she had tied up a large bundle of firewood, Hallabu told his younger brother Shadusa to take the wood to the edge of the forest.

When they could no longer hear the swish-swish of his footsteps as he carried his heavy load towards the clearing, Hallabu was suddenly overcome by feelings of jealousy towards his sister. In a rage, he slung his young sister

over his shoulder and started climbing to the top of a tall tree. The young girl
was so afraid that tears welled in her eyes and her body became stiff with
fear. If she struggled to free herself from her brother's tight grip she might fall
out of the tree and die, so she tried to keep as still as she could while Hallabu
climbed higher and higher up the tree.

With determined movements he tore off the branches that were in his way
and perspiration poured down his face. When he was nearly at the top of the
tree, Hallabu bound his young sister to one of the highest branches with a
rope of creeper that had entwined itself around the branches of the tree.
Quickly he climbed down the tree and ran off to look for Shadusa.

The young girl was so shocked that she fainted and she did not hear
Hallabu racing through the forest shouting for their brother. 'Shadusa! Come
quickly! Shadusa, come and help me find our sister. She has wandered off
and Father will be so angry with us if she is lost.'

Hallabu found Shadusa at the edge of the forest. 'Which way did she go?'
Shadusa asked.

Hallabu pointed in the opposite direction and they both went off to look for the girl. After hours of searching when all they could hear was the swish-swish of their footsteps on the forest floor, the creaking of the large trees as the wind eased them this way and that, and the hissing of leaves, they decided that they had no other choice but to go back home and tell their father that their sister was missing.

'Why did you not protect her?' their father shouted angrily. 'Why was she gathering firewood in the forest? That is your task, my sons!'

Hallabu and Shadusa looked down at the ground in front of them.

'Go back to the forest at sunrise tomorrow and search and search until you find her!'

As the first light fell on the cultivated fields in the valley below their house, the boys set out to find their sister. Hallabu searched half-heartedly while Shadusa looked everywhere, trying to find her. When they could not find her, their father's anger grew. He became more and more furious.

Meanwhile the young girl had recovered from fainting. She watched anxiously as the shadows lengthened in the forest and she was very afraid of being there alone at night. As she tried to free herself from the creeper rope that bound her tightly to the tree, she thought she heard the sound of voices, which became louder and louder.

When she looked down she saw a group of traders walking through the forest with their donkeys, which were heavily laden with kola nuts.

SIBLING RIVALRY

She shouted out loudly:

'Someone please save me! Someone please save me!'

The traders who were deep in conversation, hesitated, then thinking that it was the wind they walked on.

'Someone save me!' shouted the young girl as loudly as she could.

Again, the men stopped and listened. 'Sounds like a bird to me!' said one of them, looking up to the top of the tree that was dark in shadow. Then he caught sight of movement high in the tree and he noticed that a young girl was waving her arms.

Without hesitation he climbed to the top of the tree and cut loose the rope of creeper that bound the girl.

'Who tied you to the tree?' he asked.

He listened attentively as the young girl told him about her jealous brother.

'You cannot return to your father's house,' said the trader. 'Your brother will try to harm you again.'

The donkeys shuffled their feet and flicked their ears as they waited.

'I will take care of you as my daughter. My wife and I have no children.'

It was a long journey and the young girl was tired by the time she reached her new home. But the childless couple treated her very well and as the days passed she grew as beautiful as the rising sun. People everywhere were in awe of her beauty.

When she reached marriageable age, her foster father declared that he would only allow the finest man to claim her as his wife.

At that time, the young girl's real father sent her brother Hallabu on a journey to find a wife. He took cowrie shells, beautiful cloths and a large basket of kola nuts that his father had given him and at dawn he departed from his father's house. He travelled for many weeks in search of a beautiful maiden until eventually late one afternoon he arrived at a village renowned for its woman of great beauty.

'Is this the home of the young woman who is as beautiful as the rising sun? Please may I see her?'

'It is,' said the old man as he greeted the stranger. Because the young man was handsome and brought many fine gifts, the trader spoke to him throughout the night, trying to discern if he was worthy of his fine daughter.

The next morning when the young woman saw the strange man she said excitedly:

'Who is this handsome man that is a visitor to our village?'

'I have travelled far to meet you,' said the young man coming towards her. 'Your beauty has made you well known.'

When he spoke, the young woman recognized her eldest brother's voice, but she said nothing. Sadly, she watched as he gave the precious gifts to her foster father as a bride price.

It was with a heavy heart that the young woman left her kind foster parents' home and started on the long journey home over rugged terrain. She did not want to leave but she did not want to be disobedient to her foster father who had given her to the young man in marriage. She walked with her eldest brother carrying the golden pestle that the trader and his wife had given her as a farewell present. Although Hallabu spoke to her and tried to engage her in conversation, she said nothing in return.

At last, when their home was in sight, the young woman felt anxious. There was great rejoicing to welcome home the newly married couple. Her real parents did not recognize her and they wondered why she was so silent.

'Surely she should be happy?' her father asked her mother. 'Why doesn't she speak?'

That evening when the first stars and the crescent moon appeared in the sky, the woman sang as she pounded grain with her golden pestle to make millet cakes for her husband. She sang very softly at first and then sang more loudly:

'How can I prove whom I am?
Will my mother and father believe me?
How can I be married to my brother?'

As she sang, tears streamed down her face and the women of the village gathered around to see why she was weeping. Then an old woman called her parents who hid around the corner and listened as she sang.

'Surely this can't be the daughter we lost?' said the girl's mother.

'I know how to prove it!' said the girl's father. 'Come with me.'

'May we see your back?' he asked the young girl. 'We think that you have a scar on your back that will prove that you are our own daughter.'

The girl cried tears of relief and embraced her real parents. The scar on her back was a reminder of the time she had rolled into the fire as a baby.

'I had forgotten all about that scar,' said the young woman excitedly. 'But now you can see for yourself that I am your real daughter.'

A large feast was organised by the young woman's father to celebrate her return. When the villagers had finished their work in the fields and the first stars brought light to the coal-black sky, fires were kindled, food was served and all the villagers danced until the sun rose the next morning. Only one person did not take part in the celebrations. Hallabu, the wicked eldest brother, was so ashamed of his actions that he disappeared with his bow and arrow and never returned home again.

- Nigeria is situated between the Equator and the Tropic of Cancer.

- More than 250 ethnic groups are found in Nigeria. There are three main groups. The Hausa (and Fulani) found mainly in northern Nigeria, the Ibo (or Igbo) found in the southeast and the Yoruba in the southwest.

- English is the official language, but Hausa is spoken in the northern regions of Nigeria.

- Crops grown by Hausa farmers include millet, sorghum, cowpeas, cassava and rice.

- *Tuwo*, a Nigerian food made from maize, corn rice or millet and served with soup is popular in the north. It is also served with vegetables and beef. Pounded yams are popular throughout Nigeria. In the Yoruba southwest, pounded yams served with a vegetable soup or *ila* (okra) are favourite foods. In the east, *eba*, a cassava-based meal is often eaten. Stews, created from red peppers and meat, are common in the south.

- Palm wine, a natural juice extraction from palm trees, is drunk throughout Nigeria, especially in the southern regions where the trees flourish.

- Beautiful indigo-dyed cloth is still produced in Kano, northern Nigeria.

- Hausa males, using communal dye pits, can still be found plying their trade, which accounted for the wealth of the ancient city of Kano.

- Indigo, one of the oldest dyes used in the textile industry before synthetic dyes, was used extensively in West Africa. Crushed leaves from indigo-bearing plants such as *Indigofera* or *Lonchocarpus cyanescens*, ash and the dried residue from old vats were used to dye cloth. After the dyed cloth had dried, the fabric was traditionally beaten with wooden beaters, which pressed the cloth and gave it a shiny glaze.

- Although it is not grown in the north, the kola nut is a popular food in that region. The Yoruba in the west grow it commercially and some is imported from Ghana.

- Kola nuts are sold by hawkers in most Nigerian towns and they symbolize hospitality and peace when they are eaten during ceremonies and on formal occasions.

- Corn-pounding songs are used by women throughout Africa to express feelings that would not be acceptable if expressed in public. The songs are performed while the woman is pounding grain in the company of other women, who hear the woman's concerns. Thus pounding sessions provide opportunities for airing grievances.

THE THREE SONS

HAUSA, NIGERIA

There was once a Chief who had three sons, of whom he was very proud. They were very different, but each one was talented in some way.

One morning as he sat in the council chamber with his councillors who were dressed in full white robes, he asked them to help him assess which of his three sons was the most talented.

'I'd really like to know,' he said. 'Let's meet at the baobab tree. My sons will join us there as well.'

As the councillors moved slowly towards the tree in the hot sun, the Chief's three sons appeared in the distance, each one astride a fine horse.

When he had silenced the crowd, the Chief said: 'Each son will ride his horse in turn. He may do whatever he chooses, but on approaching the baobab tree, he must prove himself as best he can.'

The councillors looked at him with anticipation of what the boys would do.

'Then we can assess who is the most talented of my sons,' said the Chief.

Hordes of people joined the councillors next to the baobab tree and chatted excitedly as they awaited the arrival of the Chief's first son.

It was not long before he approached the crowd on his fine black horse, which kicked up the dust with its thundering hooves. Then the Chief's first son rode determinedly towards the baobab tree, travelling in a straight path. With a sharp thrust of his spear, the rider stabbed the tree with such strength that it gouged out a hole right through the trunk of the tree. Then he rode straight through the hole on his horse, stopping only when he had reached the other side.

The crowd gasped at such a display of strength and clapped as they saw the first son bring his horse to a halt and pat it on the flanks.

Then it was the turn of the second son. As the people beside the baobab tree chattered and waited in eager anticipation of the next feat, the boy came nearer, riding his horse on the dry earth, its hoof marks forming a tattoo. Then all of a sudden the horse of the second son took off and cantered straight for the tree, leaving a trail of dust. For a while the people were afraid as they thought that he would ride right into the tree and meet his death.

But as they approached the baobab, the horse and rider leapt into the air and climbed ever higher until they had cleared the tree. The people stared up at the cloudless blue sky in amazement, watching the rider and horse coming down to earth with a thump. The horse stumbled and it looked as though the Chief's son and his mare would both fall, but they steadied themselves. Then the son jumped off his horse proudly, wiping his sweaty face and hands.

With expectations raised, the crowd jostled as they awaited the arrival of the Chief's third son on his stallion. They had seen two amazing feats. Strongly he rode straight towards the baobab tree, urging his horse on. Then suddenly, when he was level with the branches of the tree, he grabbed them with his bare hands and pulled and pulled until he had unearthed the whole tree, exposing its roots to the air.

The crowd looked on in silent disbelief as he uprooted the tree. Then the Chief's third son dusted off his hands and galloped towards his father as the crowd clapped with thunderous applause. They were in awe of the performances of the three talented sons.

Who do *you* think was the most talented son?

Each son performed an amazing feat and it would be difficult to say who was the most talented son. This folktale highlights the fact that every individual has unique talents, which can be undervalued when individuals constantly compare themselves with others.

- The baobab tree is found in hot, dry savannas in Africa, Madagascar and northern Australia.
- It has a large trunk (with a maximum diameter of about 19 metres around the trunk). A hollowed-out trunk can be used to store water or grain and it can also provide shelter.
- It is sometimes called the 'upside-down tree' because of its unusual root-like branches. It can grow to a height of about 24 metres.
- Baobabs live for a long time. Some specimens are said to be about 3 000 years old and the baobab can survive long periods without water.
- The baobab tree has many uses. The bark is used in the manufacture of cords, sacks, clothing, fish nets and baskets. The leaves are used as a vegetable, similar to spinach, while its seeds are eaten raw or roasted by humans and animals. Water is added to the dried fruit pulp to make a drink similar in taste to lemonade. When fermented it becomes a traditional brew. The seeds are a rich source of vitamin C. Elephants also strip the tree of its bark.
- Soap, necklaces, glue, rubber, medicine and cloth are also made from parts of the tree.
- The baobab tree features in myths of the Bushman (San) and the Hausa of northern Nigeria. Often the baobab tree is the venue for villagers to meet to discuss communal issues and the daily news, as well as providing the venue for storytelling.

ADZANUMEE, THE BEAUTIFUL DAUGHTER

WEST AFRICA

On the west coast of Africa, north of the Equator and south of the Tropic of Cancer, lived a woman who was very unhappy. Her greatest desire was to have a daughter. Her childless state caused her great misery, even on feast days when everyone was happy and celebrating.

'I long for a daughter to be part of my life,' she said to one of her friends. 'She would give me great joy.'

One harvest time when she was pulling yams out of the ground, she unearthed one that was finely shaped. Shaking off the soil and examining it carefully with her long fingers she said aloud: 'If only this were a daughter.'

She was amazed when the long, straight yam replied: 'If I turn into your daughter, do you promise not to insult me because I was once a yam?'

The woman could not believe what she was hearing.

'Yes,' she said excitedly as she continued to stare at the yam with its unusual form.

At that moment, the long yam was transformed into a young girl.

The woman could not believe what she was seeing as she looked at the shapely, well-formed young girl emerge.

'You are so beautiful,' she said. 'You will be called Adzanumee.'

The energetic young girl became her mother's helper and made her very happy. She made bread for the household, weeded and harvested the yams in season and then took them to the busy marketplace to sell.

One such morning, Adzanumee left home at first light with her basket of yams and journeyed on foot to the market. She enjoyed the company of the

people who were there to sell their wares and after trading she chatted with friends in the dappled shade of a large tree that formed an arch overhead.

Meanwhile her anxious mother was so worried because Adzanumee had not returned home and she said: 'Where is that daughter of mine? Where is Adzanumee? She is not worthy of that special name.' She searched here and there for her and she gazed towards the hills in the far distance, but still she did not see her daughter. Disgruntled, she said: 'After all, she is only a yam!'

A bird that was partially hidden by the leaves of the tree in the woman's yard heard her words and flew rapidly off to the marketplace. It flitted around the stalls looking for Adzanumee until it found rest in the tree above her that was being swayed by a gentle breeze.

Adzanumee continued to laugh with her friends and did not notice the bird as it hopped restlessly from branch to branch in the tree above her, until it began to sing:

'Adzanumee! Adzanumee!
I've heard the words of your mother.
She says that you are not worthy of that name
Because you are only a yam!'

Adzanumee was shocked into silence. She picked up her empty basket and immediately left her friends in the shade. As she hurried along the dusty track that led to her home, she did not even see the beautiful sun as it slid down to its resting place in the west. Her eyes were filled with tears and she was both hurt and angry.

As she approached the yard at dusk, her mother ran out to greet her.

'Adzanumee, my daughter, why didn't you come home earlier? I have been so worried about you. Where have you been?' Her face showed the worry that she felt in her heart.

Seeing the tears streaming down Adzumee's face, the woman put her arm around her daughter and tried to comfort her. But her body was stiff and she moved quickly away from her mother.

'Mother, mother, you called me a yam and you said that I was not worthy of my name!' Her mother was stunned by her daughter's words and did not know how to respond.

She watched helplessly as Adzanumee put down her empty basket and walked off along the well-worn path in the direction of the fields.

The woman was so dismayed and worried that she walked quickly after Adzanumee, finding it difficult to keep to the path in the fading light.

'Stop, Adzanumee! Stop, Adzanumee!' she cried.

But Adzanumee strode on down the hill towards the yam fields. Nothing could stop her. Her mother became more and more anxious with every step.

Clasping her hands tightly she shouted: 'Don't believe that my daughter, Adzanumee! Don't believe that!' she cried. 'You are my only daughter. The one I wanted so desperately.'

Adzanumee continued down the hill and did not look back.

But it was too late. As her mother sang her sad song, Adzanumee was transformed in front of her eyes. She watched in horror as her precious daughter turned back into a yam.

When the woman came to her senses, the shapely yam was lying in the semi-darkness at the edge of the field. She wept and tried to talk to the yam, but nothing that she did could change the situation. Nothing could bring her daughter back to her. The daughter that she had wanted so desperately was the one she had chased away.

HOW YAMS CAME TO THE ASHANTI

ASHANTI, GHANA

One hot day, a traveller who was journeying through the Ashanti region showed a yam to a local man, called Abu. It is said that there were no yams in Ashanti at that time and sometimes the people were without food.

'If only we could grow yams,' Abu said to his friends, 'then when drought comes we could still have something to eat.'

The traveller explained that after harvesting the vegetable could last for months, so Abu decided to try and find yams for his people to plant. He planned his journey and then, taking weapons for his protection, he set off in search of the vegetable.

Travelling on foot, he asked the people living in the lands through which he journeyed if they knew where the country was where he could find yams. At times they pointed in one direction and at other times they directed him in the opposite way. But at last, having travelled many kilometres, he found the country where yams grew.

Looking out at the fields where the climbing yam plants with their edible tubers grew abundantly, Abu became very excited. He was so eager to acquire them that he asked the people of that country to show him where the King lived. Then when he arrived at the house of the ruler, Abu said: 'We have no yams in Ashanti. Our people are hungry because they do not have food. If you give me some of your valuable crop, I could take the yams back to my country and plant them, and thus prevent starvation.'

'Give me time to think about it,' said the King. 'But, young man, you may stay in my guesthouse.'

After a few days the King summoned Abu. Pacing up and down he said: 'It would be good to assist your people, but when they are well fed and strong, they might want to wage war against their neighbours who are not so strong.' The King looked anxious as he spoke.

'Don't be worried,' Abu said to the King. 'By nature, my people are peace loving, so you would not have this problem. I know that hungry people go to war and use conflict as a way out of their distress, but if my people were well fed there would be no need for war.'

'Ah! I see that you are a man with great plans, Abu. It might be too risky to assist you,' added the King.

Abu looked dejected. He wanted nothing more than to bring food to his hungry people. The King was silent for a while and then, scratching his chin, he said: 'If you send me one of your men to stay here as a hostage, I will assist you with the yams.'

Now Abu was one of many sons. He travelled quickly back to his father and said: 'Please, father, could you offer one of your sons to the King of the country where yams grow? The young man will stay there as a hostage, but we would be able to bring a vegetable back to this country that would prevent our people from starving.'

But Abu's father could not bear to part with any of his sons and refused to release any of them for this purpose.

'Can you imagine me sending one of my sons as a hostage?' said Abu's father. Abu then went to his brothers and asked if any of them were prepared to offer their sons for this cause. But all declined.

Showing great determination, Abu then journeyed from the place of the Ashanti and went back to the King to explain that he could not find anyone to send as a hostage.

'Without collateral I cannot offer you the yams,' said the King.

The young man Abu was crushed. He was acting in the best interests of the Ashanti people, yet they would not cooperate with him.

On his long journey home in the sweltering heat, Abu suddenly thought of approaching his sister.

'Abu,' she cried. 'I only have one son. I would be childless if my son were to go to the yam country. You are young, Abu, but if you had a child, you would understand why I am reluctant to send him.'

'Then I can do nothing about the situation,' said Abu, disappointed. 'Bringing yams back to this country would really help to alleviate hunger.'

Abu's sister listened to her brother attentively and when she realized that the yams would improve the lives of so many people, she unselfishly agreed to let her son go. Once again Abu undertook the journey and when he returned to the King with his sister's son, the King took the boy into his own home. And Abu was delighted when the King gave Abu the yams as an exchange.

Carrying the yam tubers with him in a large, wide bowl, Abu hurried back to the Ashanti people. They quickly planted the yams in rock hard, dry soil and waited for the rains to bring them to life. When the first rains fell on the parched land, the vines put out leaves as a sign of growth and the people became very excited. And in time there were so many yams planted by the Ashanti that they became one of the most important crops in that region.

Abu then decided that because his father and brothers refused to send a son, he would not have contact with them anymore.

'My sister did this noble thing,' Abu told a friend. 'She gave her son so that we all could be kept from starvation, so I will honour her.'

'How?' asked Abu's friend.

'On my death, all my property will become the right of her son who went to live in the country of the yams so that we, the Ashanti, could eat.'

And so it was that when Abu passed away, his sister's son, not his own son or brothers, inherited his land and cattle.

The Ashanti people exclaimed: 'What a wonderful thing Abu has done in bringing yams to the Ashanti. In memory of this event we will do the same.'

From that day onwards, when an Ashanti man dies, his sister's sons inherit his possessions.

In reverence to Abu, the Ashanti use the term *abu-su* to refer to their family, which means 'borrowed from Abu'.

This tale explains how, according to Ashanti tradition, boys inherit property from their maternal uncles, rather than their fathers.

- Ghana is situated a few degrees north of the Equator on West Africa's Gulf of Guinea.

- English is the official language. Other languages spoken include Ewe, Ga, Twi and Fante.

- Volta Lake, which extends from southeast Ghana to the town of Yapei in the north (about 500 kilometres), is the largest man-made lake in the world.

- The Ashanti of the Akan ethnic group is the largest group in Ghana.

- The Ashanti are known for their brightly coloured kente cloth, which is woven in narrow strips. Weaving is the exclusive domain of the men and it takes place outdoors.

- In Ghana, the history of kente cloth goes back to the twelfth century and it was worn for special ceremonies by kings and queens. It derives its name from *kenten*, which means 'basket', because its weave is similar to that of a basket. The cloth was hand-woven on looms that produce approximately ten-centimetre-wide strips of cloth. The strips are then stitched together to make wider pieces of fabric that are suitable for both men and women to use.

- The kente woven cloth is called *nwentoma* and it is different from the *ntoma* cloth that is factory produced.

- The Ashanti are also known for their hand-carved wooden stools, which are used for both sacred and domestic purposes.

- Kumasi, the ancient capital of the Ashanti kingdom, was one of the most advanced cities in Africa in the seventeenth and eighteenth centuries. Manhyia Palace, also known as Asantehene's Palace is the palace of the highest Ashanti ruler. The palace is modest (the Ashanti kings were not pretentious) and the present-day king lives in a palace behind this one. Craftsmen living around Kumasi are goldsmiths, wood carvers, weavers and cloth printers.

- About 95 per cent of the yams grown in the world are at present grown in sub-Saharan Africa. There are over 600 yam species in the world, but there are three main species grown in West Africa: the white, yellow and the water yam. The yam is one of the staple foods in West Africa.

- Soup, groundnuts or palmnuts, eaten with a starch such as *fufu* (yam, cassava, plantain or manioc), are staple foods in Ghana.

THE MAN IN THE MOON

WEST AFRICA

The man in the moon and his wife, Atai, ruled the sky when the sun disappeared and night replaced day.

Atai was the most visible of all the stars that were scattered across the night sky. When the other stars took their positions around her, they marvelled at her brightness and commented that she was as brilliant as the moon. They also thought that she was more useful, because ships and travellers on land could set their course by her position and that of the other stars.

They thought that the moon was less useful as he only gave light to the earth below and travelled through the sky. When the man in the moon heard their views he was jealous as he had been in the sky long before ships were built and travellers roamed the lands.

Then he became angry and decided that he would not shine at all or even allow the stars to brighten the night sky. But he couldn't do this on his own, so he enlisted the help of rain, thunder and lightning.

'The stars have become too proud!' he told them. 'They think that they rule the night sky and they deserve to be taught a lesson! Please, will you help me to do this?'

After much persuasion, the moon won the cooperation of the elements. Thunder roared in the heavens, streaks of lightning lit up the sky and the rain pelted down onto the land. Darkness covered the land and the rivers flooded, causing havoc on the earth. Trees, birds and animals were swept away and people sought refuge in caves and on mountain tops, experiencing great hardship and they wondered what had happened to the weather.

Many days went by. Because of the climate change, the people on earth were without food and they were cold because of the darkened skies and absence of the sun to warm them and make their crops grow.

The man in the moon was not upset by what he saw happening down on the ground. He was pleased because his wife, Atai, and the stars could not shine and he gloated over them.

Meanwhile Atai became angry as she watched the flooding continue. Although she couldn't shine, she was pleased with the fact that her husband couldn't give light either. But they were both frustrated because they could not do what they were created to do. Meanwhile, the elements were overjoyed because never before had they exerted such influence.

But on the earth, man suffered as a result. Although people prayed, some blamed each other for what was happening and they began arguing amongst themselves, creating conflict.

When night blanketed the earth, the people in caves had to keep fires burning all night to chase away the wild animals that threatened them. Every night they could see the luminous eyes of lions, hyaenas and leopards lying in wait just beyond the firelight. Normally these animals would not attack men, but their prey was becoming scarce and they were growing thin and desperate without food.

After a time, the stars became very worried about the situation and pleaded with Atai to reconsider her position and reconcile with her husband.

'It's important to have harmony between the moon and the stars,' they said. Then they suggested that when the moon was full and at its most brilliant, they could be less prominent and stay in the background. Then when the moon was less prominent the stars could shine brilliantly, having the sky to themselves and the moon could be in the background.

'Please do something, Atai,' they pleaded. 'If the elements persist, there'll be no light on the earth and perhaps no earth.'

But Atai did not take much interest in their proposals and she was not prepared to do anything about it herself. She did, however, allow them to go to the man in the moon and try to make peace on her behalf.

The man in the moon welcomed the stars as he too had become unhappy with the situation. He was no longer in charge of the night sky and he no longer had a wife. Although he pretended to show little interest in their suggestions, he said: 'I'm pleased you have come to visit me. I am definitely the ruler of the night sky, but I do not want this argument to continue.'

The stars listened carefully to him as he continued: 'I am willing to remain in the background, but I have responsibilities to the earth, as it needs my light. If this argument continues, the earth will suffer even more.'

'That's unselfish of you,' replied the stars.

At last an agreement was reached with the moon. But a problem arose with the elements. They were not eager to give up control of the sky, but eventually an arrangement was made between the three of them.

At times the moon would shine and the stars would fade into the background. When the moon shone less intensely, the stars would shine brightly, advancing to the foreground. But there would also be a time when there would be darkness so that the rain and storms could reign.

Eventually, having settled their differences, the man in the moon and his wife became friends once again and they have remained close ever since.

Some people on the earth love to see a full moon riding the night sky. Others love the brilliance of the stars, especially sailors who navigate by the position of the stars.

As for the elements, people prefer gentle rain. They are dismayed when storms and flooding sweep across the land. People and their animals are frightened by the sound of thunder and lightning, but man has come to accept all weather conditions, as they all are necessary for the benefit of the earth.

- Like the sun, the moon rises and sets every day. Its times are determined by the phase of the moon and it rises approximately thirty to seventy minutes later every day.
- From the earth, the moon is illuminated to some extent by the sun.
- There are eight traditionally recognized phases of the moon.
  - At new moon the moon is not visible (except during a solar eclipse), as the sun does not illuminate the side of the moon that faces the earth.
  - At waxing crescent, less than half the moon is illuminated by direct sunlight.
  - The first-quarter or half moon shows half the moon illuminated by the sun.
  - The waxing gibbous is slightly fuller than the half moon and occurs between the half moon and the full moon.
  - At full moon the moon seems to be totally illuminated by the sun (the moon's lit side is facing the earth).
  - The waning gibbous occurs between the full moon and the last quarter, when the moon seems to be illuminated more than a half but less than full by the sun.
  - At last-quarter or half moon the moon is half-illuminated by the sun.
  - At waning crescent, the sun illuminates less than half the moon.
- The number of bright stars that occur in the southern and northern hemispheres is almost the same.
- The Southern Cross and Centaurus are circumpolar constellations that appear in the southern hemisphere. Circumpolar constellations are those that never sink below the horizon, but change their aspect during the night. The circumpolar constellations in the northern hemisphere include Ursa Major and Cassiopeia.
- The northern hemisphere has a feature that the southern hemisphere lacks. It is a 'pole star' called the North Star or Polaris, situated directly above the North Pole. There is no star close to the South Pole.
- Early explorers such as Columbus experimented with and used celestial navigation when sailing. This means that they used the sun, moon and stars to measure their latitude.

THE TALE OF A WEALTHY MAN

TOGO

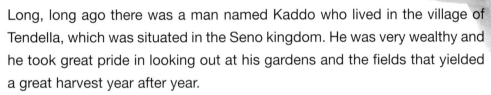

Long, long ago there was a man named Kaddo who lived in the village of Tendella, which was situated in the Seno kingdom. He was very wealthy and he took great pride in looking out at his gardens and the fields that yielded a great harvest year after year.

The men who lived in the village helped to clear the fields and turn the earth, while the women sowed seeds for Kaddo at planting time. The weather was favourable and Kaddo reaped such a good harvest that he built many granaries to store all his grain.

People who met Kaddo when they passed through Seno on their travels could not believe that he owned so much food. Soon he became well known even beyond the borders of the kingdom.

Because Kaddo had so much grain in storage, he summoned the villagers together to discuss what he should do with all the grain.

'As you can see, my granaries are filled to overflowing. My own relatives cannot eat all this food. What do you think should be done with it?'

The people thought deeply and then a wise man said: 'It is clear to me. You own so much millet and more from your fields are added to it all the time. I think that you should give some of your grain to those families here in the village for whom life is difficult when they have nothing to eat.'

Kaddo looked agitated and replied in a loud voice. 'No, I do not like that idea.' He did not want to share his grain.

The villagers discussed the matter among themselves and then one made the suggestion that Kaddo should lend grain to those people who did not

have any to plant. When they harvested their crop, they would be able to repay him.

'You would be highly regarded if you did that,' said the villager, 'and it would help to prevent poverty.'

Kaddo considered the proposal, but quickly said: 'No, that it is a bad suggestion.' Kaddo was not willing to share what he had with others.

Then another villager spoke up from the crowd. 'You could always sell some of your millet and buy some cattle. Then your granaries would not be so full.'

Kaddo was very indignant. 'That would not be right,' he said angrily.

Although many villagers made proposals, none were acceptable to Kaddo. Most of them required him to give away some of his wealth, which he did not want to do.

The sun had already started on its journey to the west when Kaddo finally announced that he would have the millet ground into meal.

'Send all the girls of the village with their mortars and pestles tomorrow,' said Kaddo. 'At first light we will grind the millet.'

The people went home dissatisfied and although they were angry, they allowed their daughters to assist Kaddo in the hope that some of the ground grain would be passed onto the villagers.

As the sun lit up the eastern sky, the women walked eagerly to their place of work. They put grain into their mortars and began pounding it with all their strength. And their songs helped them complete their task. They worked like this for seven days and each day the pile of grain grew higher and higher.

'Please, fetch water from the spring,' said Kaddo when the millet had been ground. Then the girls mixed the water with the grain as instructed, and millet bricks were made from the meal. They placed them in the sun to dry out and harden.

Kaddo was very pleased with himself. 'When the bricks are ready, I will build a magnificent wall around my house,' he said proudly.

But when the villagers heard his plan they stormed to his house to voice their disapproval of his plans.

'We have never heard of a man building a wall of millet around his home. Kaddo, you cannot use food in this way. So many people are hungry.'

Kaddo stared angrily at them and was very displeased.

'No-one in our history has created a wall out of valuable food,' they continued, trying to reason with him.

Rage grew in Kaddo. 'This grain belongs to me and I may do with it what I want. It is my right.'

When the bricks were bone dry, Kaddo instructed the people to build the wall around his house. Brick by brick, it grew. He examined it when it was waist high and continued to do so until it was eye level and he could not see the countryside beyond it. When it was completed, the people decorated it with cowrie shells.

'I will become well known because of this amazing millet wall,' observed Kaddo proudly.

The people of the village were shocked and his actions did not help him to find favour with them. But he was a wealthy man and continued to be very influential. When visitors arrived, they had to stand by the gate in the wall and wait to be invited in to see him. When Kaddo gave the villagers their instructions, he sat on the high wall so that they would have to look up at him as he addressed them from his lofty position.

News of Kaddo's wall spread like the flames of a hot and hungry fire and he became even better known.

Life continued like that until one year drought held the kingdom of Senno in its tight grip. Day after day and night after night no rain clouds gathered in the sky to water the landscape below. The fierce sun baked the earth until it was iron hard and no grain grew in it. Despite having so many fields, Kaddo harvested no grain at all.

After a while, Kaddo and his family were forced to eat the grain that they had set aside for planting. The drought continued into the next year and the next and Kaddo had to buy seed for planting. But it was no use as the dry season persisted and eventually Kaddo was forced to sell his fine horses and cattle in order to provide food for his family.

So it was that year after year no grain grew in Tendella and many of Kaddo's relations went to live in other parts of the kingdom of Seno. Kaddo could no longer keep any servants, as he could not afford to feed them. One by one

the people left the village until only Kaddo, his daughter and his donkey remained in that lonely place.

One day when hunger roared loudly in his stomach, Kaddo peeled off a little millet meal from the wall and ate it hungrily. Everyday he did the same until, after a while, the wall became lower and lower as brick by brick it was consumed. Then there was no wall left at all and the cowries lay abandoned on the ground.

Kaddo wondered where he would find food. Because of his selfish attitude when he had plenty of food, the people in the area wanted nothing to do with him.

Then one night as Kaddo was lying anxiously awake, he thought of Sogole, the King of Ghana, who was a very kind-hearted man.

Because Kaddo and his daughter were desperate they mounted their donkey and travelled for seven long, hot days until they reached the palace of Sogole. The King agreed to see him and they sat on a skin on the ground drinking millet beer. While Kaddo described the terrible drought to Sogole, he could only take small sips of the liquid, as his stomach was not used to drinking or eating anymore.

'I see that life has been difficult for you in Tendella,' said Sogole. 'We have plenty here so I will give you what you require.'

The King then asked Kaddo to tell him more about Tendella. 'I know that the drought drove people away. But I did hear about a very wealthy man who lived in Tendella. I think he was called Kaddo. Is he still living?'

'Yes,' replied Kaddo quietly.

'I heard that he built a wall of millet bricks around his house and that he spoke to people from the top of the wall. Is this the truth?'

'Yes. He did build a wall of millet around his house.'

'Is he still wealthy?' asked Sogole.

'No, he has lost everything, including the wall. Only his daughter remains.'

'What a sad state of affairs,' said the King. 'Are you a relative of Kaddo?'

'Yes, I am member of Kaddo's family. I had granaries full of grain and cattle and I was very wealthy. In fact, I am Kaddo.'

'You are Kaddo?' asked the King, disbelievingly.

'Yes. I was a man of means and influence, but now I am a beggar, asking for assistance.'

'How can I be of assistance to you?'

'King of Ghana, please give me some seed so that I can return to my home at Tendella and replant my fields.'

Sogole arranged bags and bags of millet seed for Kaddo, which were fastened to Kaddo's donkey. Kaddo was so grateful. He said farewell to the King and he and his daughter began the long journey home.

On the way home, Kaddo was nearly overcome with hunger. He was so famished that he could not continue with his travels. He took some of Sogole's seed from the sack to eat and shared it with his daughter. Because they were so hungry, they ate more and more, stopping all along the way to Tendella to eat.

When they arrived at their dusty home, they fell into an exhausted sleep. When they awoke, they ate again and again and it did not matter to Kaddo that the millet grain was for planting. Eventually he became so ill that he lay on his bed, writhing with stomach cramps and, alas, he died.

The descendants of Kaddo still reside in the Seno kingdom but they battle to make ends meet. They often refer to those who have experienced favour, but refuse to share it in the following way: 'What is the sense of building a wall of millet meal around one's home?'

- The population of Togo (Togolese Republic) is over 5.5 million people.

- The capital city is Lome.

- When Togo gained independence in 1960, Sylvanus Olympio took office. In 1963 he was deposed in a military coup. Nicolas Grunitzky, a civilian, succeeded him, but four years later he was deposed. In 1967 Gnassingbé Eyadéma became president. He was re-elected in 2003. Gnassingbé Eyadéma died in Feb 2005 and his son Faure Gnassingbé was appointed president by the military. Parliament changed the Constitution, enabling Faure to hold office for the remainder of his father's term. As this was controversial, elections were held and on 24 April 2005 Faure Gnassingbé was elected president of Togo.

- The two largest ethnic groups are the Ewe who live mainly in the south and the Kabye, who live in central and northern Togo, many of whom are terrace farmers.

- French is the official language, but both Ewe and Kabye are widely spoken.

- This small sub-Saharan economy relies on both commercial and subsistence farming. Cotton, coffee and cocoa provide export earnings.

- Phosphate mining operates in a competitive world market.

- Most food in Togo is served with a sauce and a starch. These include rice, pate (made from yams, millet, corn or manioc). One of the most popular meals is rice served with peanut sauce. Regional specialities include fresh fish sauce, *aglan* (crab) and *gboma* (spinach) along the coast. Fried yams and grilled chicken with chilli sauce are part of street cuisine. A well-known food is *fufu*, which is made by boiling chopped yams until soft, then pounding them in a mortar with a thick, strong stick until they resemble dough. *Fufu* is then eaten with a peanut, palm nut or goat sauce.

THE WOODCUTTER OF GURA

ETHIOPIA

Early one morning as the first birds broke the stillness of the night, a man from the village of Gura went out to chop firewood for his home. As there were no trees left near the village, he journeyed towards the plain and then down towards the Adi Gulgul River.

Carrying his axe, he walked along the river bank looking for wood until he saw a large dead olive tree at the water's edge. The woodcutter was delighted to have found it because it would provide a large amount of firewood for his household.

Skilfully, the man climbed the dead olive tree and sat on one of its strongest and largest branches that stretched out over the muddy waters of the river. Taking his axe, he began to chop away at the branch on which he sat. As he was chop-chopping the wood he saw a priest in the distance who was from a village not too far away.

When he came nearer, the priest looked up at the woodcutter and said:

'Why are you up the tree?'

'Can't you see that I am chopping firewood?' he said.

'Well,' said the priest, 'that is not the way to do it.'

'It's the only way to do it,' replied the woodcutter, carrying on with his chopping. 'If you want firewood, you chop the wood with your axe,' he added.

'Oh!' said the priest. 'But first you need to chop down the whole tree.'

The woodcutter listened carefully to the words of the priest as he explained: 'If you sit on the same branch that you are chopping, you'll fall out of the tree and die!'

'I don't agree with you,' said the woodcutter from Gura. 'When you want firewood, you chop it with your axe.'

The priest did not delay any longer and he hurried on his way, leaving the woodcutter sitting in the tree chopping the branch. As the sun rose higher in a cloud-streaked sky and its light shone through the bare branches of the dead tree, the woodcutter thought how foolish the priest's suggestion had been.

Suddenly there was a creak, and before he knew what was happening, the branch had broken off and the woodcutter fell, landing on the earth below with a thud. He lay sprawled on the ground with the olive branch across his chest and he remembered the words of the priest: 'He said that I would fall out of the tree and die! The branch has broken off the tree just as he said it would, therefore I must be dead as well.'

Because he thought that he had died, the woodcutter just lay motionless on the ground and didn't try to get up again.

The sun shone with bright intensity and it was midday when some of the woodcutter's friends from the village passed by. They were shocked to see him lying on the ground with a branch on top of him. They spoke to him and shook his body, but he did not respond because he thought he was dead.

They put the branch to one side and when they raised him to his feet, he fell over again because a man who has died cannot stand up. The villagers then thought that the woodcutter had indeed died and they lifted him up onto their shoulders and decided to take him back to his home in the village of Gura.

They walked slowly because of the weight they were carrying and they hadn't gone far when the woodcutter said: 'What about my axe?'

One of his friends turned around and went to fetch the axe and as they journeyed towards the village they commiserated with each other, talking about the terrible thing that had happened to their friend.

By mid-afternoon they had reached a fork in the road and as they were uncertain about which route to take from there, they stopped to rest.

'I think we should take the track along the river,' said one of the villagers.

'No, I think we should go over the hill,' said another.

An argument broke out as to which way to go and eventually the woodcutter who was still being carried on the shoulders of his friends, sat up and said: 'Take the track that goes over the hill. I came that way!'

Closing his eyes, he lay down once again and allowed himself to be carried by his friends. As they climbed up the steep hill, the villagers stopped arguing and again they discussed the misfortune of their friend, the woodcutter.

'He was right,' said one of the villagers. 'This is the shortest way. The woodcutter was so honest.'

On the other side of the hill, as they were passing the church, the priests rushed out to see what had happened and the villagers put the woodcutter on the ground.

'We found him at the olive tree near the river,' said a villager. 'A branch fell on top of him and he died.'

THE WOODCUTTER OF GURA

'No, that's not what happened!' said the woodcutter, opening his eyes. 'I was sitting on one of the branches in the tree and it broke.'

The priests shook their heads in sympathy as the friends raised the man to their shoulders again.

When they finally arrived at the woodcutter's house, there was no-one at home. They put him down and argued about what they should do next. A dog came by with his tail wagging and licked the woodcutter's face.

'Get away!' he said. 'You need to have some respect for someone who has died.'

Everyone was confused and when the dog had been driven out of the home, the arguing continued.

Suddenly the woodcutter sat up and said: 'Get my wife. She's probably at the spring. Gossiping, no doubt!'

Then he fell back down again and closed his eyes as his friends sent a message for his wife to return. Before long his wife and her friends ran back to the house, crying as a result of what they had heard. The people of the village filled the small house until they overflowed into the yard and the villagers explained to everyone what had happened.

'It was a large branch from an olive tree by the river that fell onto this man and struck him dead.'

'No, ' said the woodcutter, 'it didn't happen like that. I was sitting on the branch of the tree when it broke. I have told you this before.'

'Of course,' they muttered. 'The woodcutter was on the branch of the olive tree and it broke. He fell out of the tree and was killed.'

Then his wife said: 'Tell me, how can my husband be dead if he is able to speak?'

'But you can see that he is dead,' said one of the villagers.

'I don't think he is dead after all,' replied his wife emphatically.

Suddenly irritated, the woodcutter raised himself up into a sitting position and said: 'When I was sitting in the olive tree by the river, the priest from Mai Nebri came by. He said that I would fall out of the tree and die. He was right. I did fall out of the tree so I must be dead.'

'Oh!' said a villager. 'The priest only saw you before you fell, not afterwards.'

'All this confusion and disagreement. When will it end?' said the woodcutter.

And with that, he got up, took his axe and left the house.

'And now?' said his wife.

'I'm going to collect wood for our fire,' he said.

'He is such a considerate man,' said the villagers. 'Even at a bad time like this he thinks of the comfort of his wife!'

THE VOICE
OF THE WIND

ETHIOPIA

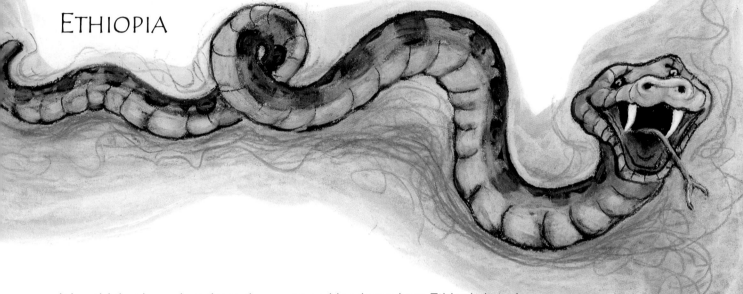

It is said that in ancient times there was no kingdom where Ethiopia is today. The land was ruled by a great serpent, Arwe, whose skin was as tough as iron and who was the length of a river. Arwe consumed all man's crops, his sheep, goats and cattle and he demanded the daughters from the inhabitants of the land. If they did not meet his demands, Arwe thrashed his tail in anger, the earth shook and boulders fell from the hills. He was greatly feared by all.

Then a stranger came to the land and through his cunning ways he was able to destroy the serpent but that is another tale that is not recorded here.

*   *   *

Long, long ago a farmer was harvesting his crop of cotton when a large snake slithered towards him.

'Please hide me!' the snake pleaded with the farmer. 'My enemies are after me and I'll be killed.'

The farmer stepped back as he was afraid and he wanted to escape. But then he said: 'Snake, although you are well known in this land for your bad deeds, in my view it is right to have compassion for one who is hunted.'

The serpent uncoiled itself under the gaze of the frightened farmer.

Then the farmer said: 'Snake, I'll hide you in that heap of cotton at the edge of my field.'

The snake had just been hidden when the hunters arrived with spears and hunting knives. Seeing the farmer, they confronted him, saying: 'Have you seen that great forest snake that devours our goats and cattle? We are out to get him!'

'No,' said the farmer.

The hunters then rushed off to continue their search for their enemy.

When the snake slid out of its warm hiding place in the pile of cotton, the farmer said: 'Now Snake, go back to your home in the forest. I don't want to see you again!'

'But I'd rather stay here,' answered the snake.

'Your life is no longer in danger,' said the farmer angrily. 'Go at once!'

But the serpent suddenly wound himself around the farmer.

'What are you doing?' cried the farmer, trying to shake off the snake.

'I am hungry,' said the snake boldly. 'I shall have to eat you.'

'Wait!' cried the farmer. 'I saved your life and now you wish to destroy me. I don't understand.'

'But I am famished,' said the snake, strengthening his grip on the farmer.

'You ungrateful creature,' shouted the farmer. 'Go away!'

'But I am hungry.'

'Well,' said the farmer, 'let our case be judged. We have to find a solution to this problem.'

The man and the snake sought the counsel of the old, gnarled sycamore tree that grew near the winding road that led to the forest. The tree listened attentively, then said: 'Farmer, I stand beside this dusty road and offer my branches as shade to all the weary travellers that pass by this way. They rest peacefully in my shadow, then rise and chop off my branches to make axes and ploughs.'

'Yes, I know that they do,' said the farmer.

'Although I am generous to man, he is very ungrateful,' said the tree. 'Therefore I cannot judge this case in your favour.'

The farmer went pale and grew very worried when the tree added: 'The snake is entitled to eat you.'

'We must get another opinion,' said the anxious farmer. So he and the snake hurried through the grassy banks of the river where the grass grew to knee height.

Then the farmer asked the river that flowed swiftly through the forest to give its opinion.

The sludge-coloured river listened to their story and said: 'Listen to me. Without a river, man could not survive. He would die if he couldn't quench his thirst with my cool waters. When there is drought, man digs holes in my banks to find water for his animals and for himself.'

'That is true,' said the farmer.

'But when it rains heavily and I can no longer contain my water, I flood my banks onto man's fields and he is angry with me. He curses me and throws stones at me.'

The farmer was silent as he looked at the muddy brown waters of the fast flowing river.

'Yes, Farmer,' the river continued, 'man forgets the good that I do for him. I have no use for man. As this is man's nature, I cannot judge in your favour.'

The farmer was shocked, but even more so when the river said: 'The snake may eat you.'

In desperation the farmer told his story to the grass that rustled in the breeze that blew across the open land. The grass listened for a long time and then said: 'Farmer, I grow silently in this valley. I give food to man's cattle and goats. Man uses me to thatch the roof of his house as a means of protection. I am very useful to him.'

'Yes,' said the farmer, agreeing with the grass.

'He even uses me to make baskets for storing his food,' continued the grass, 'and I continue to grow more for him.'

'That is correct,' said the farmer, trying again to shake off the snake.

'But what happens then?' queried the grass. 'When I am old and a little tough, man burns me. He plants grain in place of me. Then he weeds me out of the way and destroys me if I grow between his rows of planted seed.'

The farmer and the snake waited for the grass's opinion.

'Man is not good,' said the grass. 'On account of this, I cannot judge in your favour, Farmer. The snake may eat you.'

'That is a cruel, harsh judgement,' ranted the farmer. He left the grass and hurried away. On the road back to the forest, which was the resting place of the great snake, they met the wind.

The farmer was without hope but he told his long story to the attentive ears of the wind who was swirling around them.

The wind considered the situation for a long while and then said: 'I see that all things live according to their nature. The grass grows to live and man burns it to stay alive. The river flows according to its nature and it cannot help overflowing its banks from time to time. It is only right for man to be angry when his fields are flooded because they are his livelihood.'

'What about the tree?' asked the farmer.

'The tree nurtures its branches both for beauty and shade, and for other uses. And no-one can blame the tree, grass or river for their judgements.'

The cotton farmer was desperate. There was no way out for him.

The wind whipped around them and continued. 'This is not a matter for judgement because all things act according to their nature. So let us dance and sing in appreciation for the way things are,' suggested the wind.

So the wind gave the farmer and the snake each a drum to play. In order to make music, the snake had to release its grip on the farmer. Then the wind sang to the snake: 'As it is your nature to eat man, eat the man!'

And the wind said to the farmer: 'As it is your nature not to be eaten, do not allow yourself to be eaten.'

'That is correct,' said the farmer, relieved.

Realizing that he was free of the snake, the tired farmer ran all the way home to his village and did not stop until he reached his cotton field.

- Ethiopia is a landlocked east African country that is situated west of Somalia. Addis Ababa is the capital city.

- The Great Rift Valley that runs through Ethiopia sometimes experiences earthquakes and volcanic eruptions. Droughts occur often in this region.

- The country has small reserves of copper, potash, platinum, gold and natural gas.

- The Oromo comprise almost half of the population and are made up of Christians, Muslims and traditional animists. Other ethnic groups include the Amhara and Tigre, Sidamo, Shankella and Somali.

- Amharic, the language of the Amhara, is the official language, but there are more than 75 languages spoken in Ethiopia.

- Almost half the country is Muslim, while the Ethiopian Orthodox Church, predominant on the central plateau, comprises about 35–40 per cent of the population.

- The Ethiopian Orthodox Church has played a significant role in Ethiopian religious society since the fourth century. It has a monastic tradition.

- Much of Ethiopia's artistic expression has been inspired by religious themes and is exhibited in churches.

- Ethiopian culture includes a naïve style of painting that is found in most churches. Two-dimensional figures with almond-shaped eyes are portrayed, using strong colour and clear lines.

- *Injera* is bread made from the grain teff, which is a staple in Ethiopia. The most favoured dishes are thick stews called *wats*, which have meat, vegetables or beans as their main ingredients. *Doro wat* is a spicy chicken dish. *Dabo kolo* are small biscuits that are fried and are very popular.

- The singing of folk songs is a popular tradition in Ethiopia. The following instruments are used: the masenko, a single stringed instrument that is played by minstrels; the krar, which has five or six strings, resembles a lyre and is plucked; and the begenna, a portable harp.

THE MAN AND THE GAZELLE

ZANZIBAR

On the island of Zanzibar, which is washed by the warm waters of the Indian Ocean, lived a poor man called Hamdaani. Often he was so desperate that he went begging for food at people's houses and at times he took things before they were given to him. When people became aware of this they shunned him, and so every morning he went to the dump in the village to look for food, hoping to find a little millet.

He was so excited one day because he found a couple of coins. He put the shiny coins in the pocket of his ragged trousers and continued to look for food as he was hungry, but he did not find any. 'At least I have some money,' he said. 'I'll just go home and have a sleep.'

The next day as the bright sun rose over the water, Hamdaani was at the village dump, foraging for food. As he sifted through the rubbish, he noticed a man passing by who carried a twig cage.

'What do you have inside there?' he asked.

'Gazelles,' replied the man, who was a trader.

'I'd like to see them. Please bring them over here.' Hamdaani's eyes lit up as the trader walked towards him.

'Don't go!' said some men standing nearby on the side on the road.

'Why not?' asked the trader.

'Oh! That man does not have any money. He scratches in the dump daily to find food to eat. If he did have money, he'd be more interested in a meal than an antelope. Don't waste your time with him!'

The trader ignored the men's comments and approached Hamdaani with the cage of gazelles. 'Here, look at them,' he said.

'What is the cost of your animals?' the poor man asked the trader. 'Could I use these coins to buy one?'

The men at the side of the road laughed scornfully at Hamdaani, but he pulled out his money and offered it to the trader.

The trader then took a small but beautiful gazelle out of the cage and gave it to Hamdaani saying: 'This one is called Kijipa.'

Hamdaani was excited as he led his animal away and he took good care of the gazelle. At night he slept next to it. But he continued to live as he had done before. A week passed and then one night Hamdaani woke up startled, thinking that he had heard a voice.

'Master! Master!'

'Who is it?' asked Hamdaani.

'It is me, Kijipa,' said the gazelle.

Hearing the gazelle speak made him nervous and he wanted to run away.

'Listen to me,' said Kijipa.

'I'm listening,' said Hamdaani.

The gazelle continued: 'You are my master, Hamdaani, and I will not leave you. You forage for a few grains of millet, but that is not enough for me. I'll die of starvation.'

Hamdaani felt guilty and looked at the ground.

'Let me go off every day to find my own food,' said Kijipa. 'I promise that I'll come back every night.'

'Alright,' said Hamdaani. He was reluctant to let the animal go, but he could not stop him looking for food.

So the next day Kijipa left the man at sunrise and returned at sunset. This happened every day until the sixth day. On that day when he was looking for food in a bushy area, Kijipa scratched at the grass that grew under a shady tree and he found a diamond. It glinted in the sunlight and caused Kijipa to exclaim: 'This is worth a fortune. If I give it to Hamdaani, someone who is after it will kill him. I think that I will offer it to a very powerful person.'

When the sun set and darkness replaced the fading light of day, Kijipa did not return to his master. He was travelling to the city where the sultan lived in his palace. After journeying all night, he arrived at the city the next morning and people commented: 'That's strange. Look at that gazelle running through the city streets carrying something in his mouth that is hidden in leaves.'

The sultan was at the palace door when the gazelle arrived and he was very surprised to see his visitor. He was even more surprised when the gazelle dropped the diamond on the ground and lay beside it.

'Good day, Master!' he cried.

'Why have you come here?' replied the sultan. 'It is not usual for a gazelle to visit me.'

Kijipa explained: 'Master, I have come to secure a family alliance with you. Would you be agreeable to that?'

'This is good timing,' said the sultan. 'I am very eager for a family alliance. Give me your proposal.'

'This is the pledge I bring, Master,' said Kijipa dropping the diamond in the sultan's lap. 'The pledge is from my master, Sultan Daaraa'ee. He knows that you are the father of a fine daughter.'

The sultan smiled and looked down at the gazelle. 'The Sultan Daaraa'ee has my permission to marry my beautiful daughter and he may come without anything as I do not want more from him. He must be a good man.'

Kijipa was so excited when he left the sultan and started on his long journey home to Hamdaani.

When he arrived home he found that Hamdaani was very angry with him as he thought that he was lost. 'I have good news,' said the gazelle.

'What is it? What is it?'

Kijipa told Hamdaani about his visit to the sultan and about his future prospects and the next day they both set off for the palace that was situated in the bustling city. On the way Kijipa made Hamdaani wash in the stream and when they passed through the forest he said: 'Let's sleep here.' Then he beat Hamdaani with a stick, which seemed strange at the time. 'I'm leaving you now,' said the gazelle. 'Do not move away.'

The gazelle journeyed to the city and when he arrived at the sultan's palace, he found a huge crowd waiting for Sultan Daaraa'ee.

As he greeted the sultan, the gazelle said: 'Sultan, I can hardly walk. I have bad news for you.'

'What is it?' asked the sultan, shocked.

The gazelle made up a tale of robbery and misfortune that had happened in the forest and explained how the Sultan Daaraa'ee had had his clothes stolen.

The sultan immediately asked for clothes to be brought to him and after selecting the finest ones, he chose a walking stick, which he gave to the gazelle. 'Take these clothes to Sultan Daaraa'ee and I will provide him with a horse as well,' said the generous sultan.

Kijipa took the fine clothes to his master in the forest and when he was dressed in them, he helped Hamdaani onto the horse.

'I cannot believe what is happening to me' said Hamdaani.

As they travelled through the countryside the gazelle said: 'Look at you, Hamdaani. No-one would ever know you were at the village dump yesterday.'

Hamdaani rode proudly into the city with the gazelle following him and very soon he was married to the sultan's daughter. A great feast was held in their honour.

Hamdaani agreed to let Kijipa go because he was so happy and wanted to spend time with his new wife.

But some time later while foraging for food in the forest, Kijipa thought about his master and wondered why he had been so hard on him, letting him

go and then making no contact with him. 'I have been so good to him, risking my life for him and giving him everything I had,' he said aloud. 'I am surprised that he never even asked me how I did it.'

Tugging at a tough clump of grass, the gazelle regretted the fact that his master had never done anything for him. 'I wish he would do something for me to show that he cares,' he said.

And then Kijipa thought of a plan. He visited the old woman who was often in the forest and said: 'Kind woman, I'm so sick. I have a fever and my body is aching. Please help me'.

'I'm sorry to hear that,' said the old woman.

'Please, could you go to my master and tell him that I need him?'

The old woman agreed and travelled a long distance to the palace in the city. There she found Hamdaani and his wife dressed in fine silks from India, sitting on the couch together.

'Kijipa is very ill and he would like to see you,' she said.

But all Hamdaani did was send some soup to him. The gazelle was very disappointed and he sent the woman back to tell his master that Kijipa was too sick to eat the soup.

When Hamdaani saw the old woman returning he stormed out to meet her and was very angry. His wife, the sultan's daughter, wept and said: 'If a man is so ungracious, it will lead to his downfall.'

'Why are you speaking to me like that?' said Hamdaani angrily. 'Why should I worry about a gazelle that cost me a few coins?'

The old woman turned her back on him and journeyed back to the forest. A wind whipped through the trees and when she found the gazelle he was weak and in a poor condition. Hamdaani's wife had sent a pillow for him and some rice, but he died of a broken heart.

When the people heard that the gazelle had died, everyone cried bitterly, even Hamdaani's wife.

'Why are you so upset? You are mourning as though *I* were dead,' he said to her. 'Only a gazelle that cost me a few coins has died.'

Hamdaani's wife was so upset by his insensitivity that she wrote to her father and asked him to fetch her.

When the sultan and all his attendants arrived, they discovered that Hamdaani had thrown Kijipa's body into a well. The sultan cried and when Kijipa had been brought up from the well, he took the body and buried it properly, showing his compassion for animals.

That night, Hamdaani's wife had a dream that she had returned to the home of her youth and when she woke the next morning she found that she was in her own bed in her own home in her own town.

Hamdaani had a nightmare. He dreamed he was searching for food at the village dump and the children were laughing at him as they passed by.

'Where have you been, Hamdaani? We thought you had died,' they said.

The sultan's daughter lived happily to the end of her days, but Hamdaani kept foraging for food in the village dump until the day he died.

- Zanzibar, Tanzania, consists of two main islands off the east coast of Africa: Zanzibar (Unguja) and Pemba. Zanzibar is the most developed island.

- Stone Town is the main economic centre on the island of Zanzibar. It is known for its carved wooden doors, narrow, winding roads and mosques. The historic buildings found there include the Palace Museum and the Old Fort, which contain clothing and furniture from the days of the sultans.

- Zanzibar's main industries are fishing, tourism and spices (cinnamon, nutmeg and pepper) and it is the world's leading producer of cloves.

- KiSwahili and English are the official languages.

- The Zanzibar Red Colobus monkey is only found in Zanzibar.

- You are able to travel to the island of Zanzibar by ferries that travel to and from Dar es Salaam on the Tanzanian mainland.

- Persian immigrants from Shiraz first settled in Zanzibar around AD 975. The Portuguese controlled the island from 1503 until 1698, when it fell under the control of the Sultan of Oman as part of his overseas holdings. In 1861 Zanzibar and Oman were split. Sayyid Majid bin Said Al-Busaid (1834–1870) became Sultan of Zanzibar and his brother Sayyid Turki bin Said Al-Busaid (1832–1888) became Sultan of Oman.

- Eventually the British Empire ruled and Zanzibar became a protectorate of the United Kingdom in 1890. British-appointed rulers called Viziers were in charge and then British Residents from 1913–1963.

- Although Zanzibar received its independence in 1963 as a Constitutional Monarchy under the Sultan, he was overthrown in 1964 and Zanzibar joined the African state of Tanganyika to become the United Republic of Tanzania.

THE GIRL WITH A GAP BETWEEN HER TEETH

Long, long ago in central Kenya, where there was plenty of grazing for cattle and goats, a beautiful young girl named Wacici lived with her family. When she smiled you could see the gap between her well-formed front teeth, which, in those parts, made her even more beautiful.

In fact, her beauty was well known not only in the area in which she lived, but in the surrounding districts as well. Everyone had heard of the beautiful Wacici. Whenever the young girls went visiting as a group they noticed that the young men only took an interest in Wacici. This made them very jealous of her and so they thought of a plan to try and get rid of her. This way, they hoped that the young men would like them instead.

One carefree summer afternoon, when all the girls of the area were on their way to visit friends, they came across an aardvark's tunnel. They quickly whispered and connived amongst themselves and decided that they would push Wacici down the tunnel.

As the wind whipped through the grass at their feet, they suddenly grabbed the beautiful Wacici and shoved her down the tunnel.

'What are you doing?' she said as they pushed her, but she was not able to stop them.

The hole was very deep and it grew darker as she went further down, down into the depths of the earth. The young girls smiled, as they knew that even if she tried, she would never be able to climb out of it. Then they continued on their way to meet their friends, dancing and singing as they went along.

Fortunately for Wacici, who was left behind in the aardvark hole, she could still breathe because when she was pushed into the tunnel she was not buried by the soil.

Wacici had a younger brother who loved her very deeply. If she had not returned home by the time the moon and his tribe, the stars, had risen in the night sky, he would stay awake waiting for her, even though he was very tired after his daily activity of herding the goats. He even had a special song that he sang to his sister. When she did not return home that night, the young boy was tearful and very worried about her safety. The next morning

when he went out with his goats he searched everywhere for her. As his energetic brown and white goats tugged at the coarse clumps of grass around him and then wandered off, he kept singing his special song for her:

'Wacici, Wacici,
You, with the gap between your teeth,
You are so beautiful.
Wacici, Wacici,
You with the gap between your teeth,
You are so beautiful.'

The wind caught his song and carried it over the hills and, as people knew that the young boy always sang for his sister, they didn't pay much attention to him as he continued to sing and sing, never giving up. Even the goats that wandered off to the rocky outcrop nearby took no notice of his song.

As he sat, gazing out over the hillside, the young boy did not suspect that Wacici was nearby. The girls knew, but they carried their secret with them as they travelled across the countryside and had anyone known what they had done, they could have been accused of murder.

Poor Wacici had been pushed headfirst into the aardvark tunnel and, although she was still living, the girls thought that she had not survived her fall. Meanwhile in the dark depths of the tunnel, Wacici heard a faint sound and then she heard singing, but she thought that it came from a long distance away. The song sounded familiar and as it became louder, she recognized the singer as her brother.

'It is my brother, the one I love deeply,' she said aloud, and for the first time hope rose within her.

Wacici was so excited that she sang the special song for her brother and as his frisky goats frolicked around him, his sister's song reached his ears. He jumped up and looked all around him as the singing continued. He looked to the left and to the right, in front of him and behind, but he couldn't hear where the singing was coming from as it was muffled.

As he walked towards the tunnel, his foot struck the mound of soil near the opening and he suddenly realized that the singing was coming from deep inside the hole. The boy looked down the tunnel in the hope of finding his sister. He was even prepared to risk his life for the sake of Wacici, but he decided that the hole was too deep. So he left his goats grazing and ran home to get help.

The people in his village could not believe the young boy's tale about Wacici. They doubted that the aardvark hole even existed, as they had never seen it before, but they followed him all the same.

As the sun was halfway on its journey to the west in a cloud-streaked sky, the boy ran to the aardvark tunnel, followed by breathless people who were struggling to keep up with him. First the older people went down the tunnel and were relieved to find Wacici. Then they tied a leather strap around her and those who remained at the entrance pulled her out of the hole. Everyone was very relieved that Wacici was rescued in time. Although she was frightened and in shock, she had survived the ordeal.

The elders discussed the young girls' behaviour, but because they all came from the same district, they decided not to punish them, saying, 'All children are the same. They all behave badly at times.'

Everyone was just so relieved that Wacici did not die nor was she harmed in any way.

Wacici grew to be even more beautiful as the years passed. When she was a young woman she married and was made a member of the clan and part of the community, as is the custom amongst the Agikuyu people. People admired her even more because she held no anger towards the girls who had caused her such pain. They even became friends again.

THE REUNION

KIKUYU, KENYA

A young man named Wagacharaibu lived with his sister in a mountainous area in central Kenya that was very isolated. Both their parents had died and they stayed alone in a house high in the hills, which had a spectacular view of the lands below, where there were waterfalls and a strong flowing river that snaked through the deep valley.

The handsome young man had strong facial features and his hair had grown so long that it reached his waist. Because of his good nature he was well liked and often went off to visit his friends. But at times like these his sister M'weru was left alone. Only the wind that roared around the mountains kept her company and occasionally she saw the crowned eagle high in the sky in search of food for its young.

One evening at dusk when Wagacharaibu returned home from being with his friends, M'weru cried to him: 'Brother, please do not leave me alone. When you were away last night three men came here, each carrying a club and spear. I was so frightened,' she said. 'Don't go away again. If you do, I know that the men will return to carry me away.'

'That would not happen,' he said.

The next morning as the sun cast its amber light onto the rocky hills and they became alive to the first birds of the day, Wagacharaibu left the house and set off on a journey to visit his friends. The day passed slowly as M'weru completed her household duties of sweeping and cooking. Later, when the sun sank behind the mountains and a strong wind circled the house causing the windows to rattle, M'weru sat fearfully inside, gazing out at the full moon

and the stars that shone out of a coal-black sky longing for her brother to return. She was lonely and afraid.

It was not long before she heard noises in the distance, which came closer until the men with the clubs and spears burst into the house, grabbed M'weru and lifted her up, carrying her away into the night.

Sometime later when Wagacharaibu returned to the empty house and searched for his sister, he could not find her. When he ran outside he thought he heard a distant voice crying faintly: 'My brother, the men have taken me away. But in our house you will find some soup.'

Wagacharaibu wondered where the words came from. Was he imagining them? He was also worried about the safety of his sister. Who would cook for him and shave the front part of his head now that his sister had gone?

The following morning, when the grass was still wet with dew, Wagacharaibu went to look for his sister. He had not gone far when he suddenly stopped. He thought he heard her voice and shouted her name loudly: 'M'weru, M'weru, where are you?' Then he listened carefully.

Meanwhile M'weru heard his deep voice as it was carried across the countryside by the wind. But the brother and sister could not find each other.

For months Wagacharaibu searched for his sister, scouring the hills and valleys in the hope that he might find her. As he walked, he shielded his face from the sun and rain with a goatskin hat that was tied under his chin with two strings.

Months turned into years as Wagacharaibu continued his search in the hills and the valleys of the Abedare Mountains. One afternoon as he was passing a large homestead, he begged food from a woman who was cooking inside. She shared some of her food with the stranger but she did not offer it in a good container, she put it on a broken piece of pot.

'Would you like to stay here for the night?' she asked, feeling sorry for him.

'Thank you,' replied Wagacharaibu. He was exhausted from the long journey over rugged terrain and his feet ached.

The next morning, when the sun rose in a pale blue sky, Wagacharaibu went to the fields some distance below the house with the woman's son to help scare the birds away from the crops. The grain was almost ready for harvest and as he threw little stones to frighten off the birds he said: 'Fly away bird, just like M'weru who will never be seen again.'

The young boy listened carefully to these words and when the stranger was not in the house, he told his mother the strange words spoken by the man.

But the woman ignored her son and when he went back to the fields the next day to help protect the grain from the birds, the stranger spoke the same strange words. On the third morning, the woman went with her son and the young man to the fields and while sitting some distance away, she heard the stranger say: 'Fly away bird, just like M'weru who will never be seen again.'

M'weru jumped up and ran across to her son and the stranger.

'Why do you speak like this to the birds?' she said.

'My sister, M'weru, went missing. I have searched for her for many months and years now, but I cannot find her.'

'Oh!' said the woman. 'Are you really my brother?' she asked, placing her bony fingers over her eyes as she wept bitterly. 'I am M'weru,' she cried, 'your sister.'

Wagacharaibu's appearance was so different from what it had been because of his time on the road that she had failed to recognize her own brother.

'You look different,' she said. 'Your hair is so uncared for and so are your clothes. I will dress you like before and I will see if you really are my brother whom I have not seen for such a long time.'

M'weru hurried to her husband who was one of the men who had carried her off so long ago and she took four sheep and three goats from his flocks. The sheep were killed and Wagacharaibu ate the meat, which strengthened him once again.

His sister took some fat and did his hair, letting it rest on his shoulders. From the two black and one white goatskins, she created a cape. Then she put a spear in his strong hand and it was the same spear that her husband had used when he had carried her off.

On Wagacharaibu's arms, M'weru placed iron and brass armlets and ornaments around his neck and legs.

'Now you really are my brother Wagacharaibu,' she said proudly.

M'weru's husband thought so highly of Wagacharaibu that he gave him three oxen and twenty frisky goats, more than a bride price for his sister. With his hands he built him a house and gave him another thirty goats with which he could seek a wife.

In time Wagacharaibu found a young woman and brought her back to his house. Wagacharaibu was so comfortable in his new life that he remained living in the same household as his sister. He planted crops in the fertile ground and traded his animals.

- Kenya is situated on the east coast of Africa with Sudan and Ethiopia to the north of it.
- The coastal area of Kenya, which includes coral reefs and islands, is very fertile. The area rises to the dry highlands, which have savanna and thornbush vegetation.
- The main tribes in Kenya are the Agikuyu (or Kikuyu), Meru, Kalenjin, Luo, Kisii, Kamba, Swahili, Maasai and Turkana. The Agikuyu comprise Kenya's largest ethnic group. They are found mainly in the central part between Nairobi and Mount Kenya.
- According to myth, the Agikuyu god, Ngai, took Gikuyu to the summit of Kirinyaga and instructed him to build his house there. He was given a wife, Mumbi, and they had nine daughters who formed the nine clans of the Agikuyu.
- In Agikuyu culture, the first boy born in a family is named after the father's father and the second after the mother's father. The first girl is named after the father's mother and the second after the mother's mother.
- Girls with a gap between their top front teeth are considered to be attractive amongst the Agikuyu.
- The Agikuyu people are agriculturalists. They farm mainly in the foothills of Mount Kenya and their crops include coffee, tea, maize, sorghum, millet and bananas.
- They owned cattle, sheep and goats and traded with the Maasai and the Kamba.
- Many Agikuyu people are very business orientated today and entrepreneurial.
- The Maasai are found mostly in southern Kenya and also Tanzania. Tradition suggests that their rain god, Ngai, gave them all the cattle for safekeeping when the earth and sky split. Thus they believe they are justified in raiding their neighbours who are not Maasai, in order to retrieve their cattle.
- The Maasai have a traditional nomadic, pastoral way of life with cattle and sheep as the basis of their economy. They live off the milk, blood and meat of their animals.
- The Maasai are distinguishable by their dress, which is often red and regarded as a symbol of power. They wear loosely fitting clothing and the beaded discs worn around their necks are made by the females. Men colour their hair with red clay from the earth and wear earrings in their lobes.
- *Ugali*, a maize meal porridge is eaten in Kenya. Other dishes include chicken cooked in coconut milk and spiced red beans.

BIBLIOGRAPHY

Arnott, K. *African Myths and Legends,* Oxford University Press, 1989.

Barker, W.H. and Sinclair, C. *West African Folktales,* George Harrap and Co, 1917.

Bourhill, E. and Drake, J. *Fairy Tales from South Africa,* MacMillan And Co, London 1908.

Callaway, Rev. C. *Nursery Tales, Traditions and Histories of the Zulus,* Reprinted by Negro
　Universities Press, 1969.

Canonici, N. *The Zulu Folktale Tradition,* University of KwaZulu-Natal Press, 1993.

Courlander, H. *A Treasury of African Folklore,* Crown Publishers, 1975.

Courlander, H. and Leslau, W. *The Fire on the Mountain and other Ethiopian Stories,*
　Henry Holt and Co, New York, 1950.

Du Toit, B. *Content and Context of Zulu Folk-Narratives,* University Presses of Florida, 1976.

Hammond-Tooke, D. *The Roots of Black South Africa,* Jonathan Ball Publishers, 1993.

Kabira, W.M. *The Oral Artist,* Heinemann, Kenya, 1983.

Lane, Y. *African Folktales,* Peter Lunn Publishers, 1946.

Leslau, C. and Leslau, W. (eds). *African Folk Tales,* Peter Pauper Press, 1963.

Postma, M. *Tales from the Basotho,* Afrikaanse Pers-Boekhandel, 1964.

Radin, P. (ed.). *African Folktales and Sculpture,* Bollingen Series, Pantheon Books, 1964.

Savory, P. *Xhosa Fireside Tales,* Howard Timmins, Cape Town, 1963.

The Best of African Folklore, Struik Publishers, Cape Town, 1988.

The Origin of Stories is sourced from http://www.canteach.ca/elementary/Africa.html

Special thanks to Joy Clack, Linda de Villiers and Beverley Dodd

First published in 2006 by Struik Publishers
(a division of New Holland Publishing (South Africa) (Pty) Ltd)
Cape Town • London • Sydney • Auckland
www.struik.co.za

Cornelis Struik House, 80 McKenzie Street, Cape Town 8001, South Africa
Garfield House, 86–88 Edgware Road, London W2 2EA, United Kingdom
14 Aquatic Drive, Frenchs Forest, NSW 2086, Australia
218 Lake Road, Northcote, Auckland, New Zealand

New Holland Publishing is a member of Johnnic Communications Ltd

10 9 8 7 6 5 4 3 2 1

PUBLISHING MANAGER: Linda de Villiers
EDITOR: Joy Clack
DESIGNER: Beverley Dodd
ILLUSTRATOR: Marjorie van Heerden
PROOFREADER: Neilah Miller

Reproduction by Hirt & Carter Cape (Pty) Ltd
Printed and bound by Kyodo Printing Co (Singapore) Pte Ltd

ISBN 1 77007 231 4

www.imagesofafrica.co.za
IMAGES OF AFRICA
PHOTO LIBRARY
Log on to our photographic website **www.imagesofafrica.co.za**
for an African experience